DETROIT PUBLIC LIBRARY

3 5674 05779271 6

D0108149

THE
OFFICIAL
REPORT
ON HUMAN
ACTIVITY

Campbell Branch Library
8733 W. Vernor
Detroit, MI 48209
(313) 481-1580

JUN - - 2018

Made in Michigan Writers Series

General Editors

Michael Delp, Interlochen Center for the Arts
M. L. Liebler, Wayne State University

Advisory Editors

Melba Joyce Boyd
Wayne State University

Stuart Dybek
Western Michigan University

Kathleen Glynn

Jerry Herron
Wayne State University

Laura Kasischke
University of Michigan

Thomas Lynch

Frank Rashid
Marygrove College

Doug Stanton

Keith Taylor
University of Michigan

A complete listing of the books in this series can be found online at wsupress.wayne.edu

THE
OFFICIAL
REPORT
ON HUMAN
ACTIVITY

Stories by kim d. hunter

WAYNE STATE UNIVERSITY PRESS
DETROIT

© 2018 by Wayne State University Press, Detroit, Michigan 48201. All rights reserved. No part of this book may be reproduced without formal permission. Manufactured in the United States of America.

ISBN 978–0-8143-4520-7 (paperback); ISBN 978–0-8143-4521-4 (ebook)

Library of Congress Control Number: 2017958522

Words and music for "The Secret" by Peter Blegvad and Anthony Moore copyright © (renewed) 1967 Pepamar Music Corp. All rights administered by WB Music Corp. All rights reserved. Used by permission of Alfred Music.

Publication of this book was made possible by a generous gift from The Meijer Foundation. This work is supported in part by an award from the Michigan Council for Arts and Cultural Affairs.

Wayne State University Press
Leonard N. Simons Building
4809 Woodward Avenue
Detroit, Michigan 48201–1309

Visit us online at wsupress.wayne.edu

Contents

The Official Report on Human Activity or Long for an Elephant

An Essay

1. Ipso in the Elephant

When Ipso gave birth to what most agreed was an elephant, there were those who tried to act as though it was normal. Well, yes, he was a man, they said, and no one had known he was pregnant, but it was, after all, a small elephant.

Prior to the birth, he had been eating strangely and spending an inordinate amount of time alone. But none around him had taken these things as signs that anything unusual was about to occur because he had said that he was a writer, or that he wanted to be a writer. He had trouble deciding which of these things to tell people, because writing happens so much in the mind that he thought it would be difficult to know when or if he had crossed the threshold. First, he would have to find something to write about.

He could write about the factory where he worked and things he and his coworkers made in the factory. He would have to start at the beginning and that would mean light in the morning. So he tried to begin with the light in his windows on the mornings he had to go to work, versus the light in his windows on the mornings he did not have to go work. The difference between daylight and worklight was much like the difference between sleep on the nights that were not followed by work days (Friday sleep and Saturday sleep) and regular sleep.

The problem was, once he began writing about the light and how he slept, it felt like he was trying to walk on slippery rocks that sloped toward quicksand, or how he imagined a slope of slippery rocks would be, as he was not much for the outdoors and tried to stay in when it rained. The fact that he could imagine these things made him lean toward saying that he was a writer as opposed to wanting to be a writer. But the fact that he had gotten his knowledge of quicksand from TV lessened his idea of himself as a writer.

2. Write What You Know

If you've worked in a more modern factory than the one where Ipso worked, one built in the twenty-first century, for example, or, if you've never worked in a factory at all, count yourself relatively lucky, especially if you have found another way to get food that is less humbling and absurd than working in a plant. Second, you may not recognize the sort of factory that Ipso worked in, as it was built earlier in the twentieth century. It was noisier and dirtier than more modern factories. It was much harder to find a place where you could be alone with whatever thoughts hadn't been purged by the noise and dirt. Perhaps, the lack of time alone with thoughts made the contemplation of light and sleep seem like a grim, endlessly narrowing spiral. He didn't want to describe it as dark because he was dark and he associated the dark with warmth, standing by the oven when the sun went down in late winter with lights dimmed and the bed waiting for him to deliver the heat his body had absorbed from the small kitchen.

He was torn between trying to describe the narrowing spiral and trying to find out where it led. He thought he should describe it because that is what writers do. He wanted to find out where it led because he was frightened and fear made him curious as though he were in a lucid, recurring nightmare. Where would a narrowing path draped in factory light lead, certainly not to a screened-in summer porch with cold beer on hand and Miles Davis playing.

He thought about Miles Davis a lot. Miles was dark like Ipso, but, having lived and died in the twentieth century, Miles was obviously older. Miles produced a tone on the trumpet of unerring beauty and played, in his second great band, with younger writers whose noise was as fitted and sculpted to jagged music as Miles's was to a clean, Jean Toomer narrative. What held Miles and those wilder, younger players together was that Miles's melody led to the same inside dark with hidden sources of illumination.

In short, they dreamt together awake, practiced hour after hour the climb on raggedy surfaces toward the edge of a cliff whose beauty would be a fantasy if not for the climb, whose beauty could only be grasped in the moments over the white ocean of clouds rolling below the sun, the moments before the plunge where the purity and cold of the air and then the cloud overcame thought and vision respectively, a fall as blind as the stasis of the womb.

Miles didn't give many interviews. Essentially, he thought it was all there in the music, no reason to talk about what everyone could hear. For Ipso, it was very strange for a writer to eschew words, even for an interview. But Ipso could still identify with Miles because he knew Miles had had difficulty getting along. He could hear it in the alone sound of Miles's trumpet and the heat beneath the loneliness, the Harmon mute at the bell of the horn honing every breath and note through a tunnel of black light to the inner ear, a path as lean and solitary as it was immutable and unforgiving, and he thought that loneliness may be the only thing he had in common with another great writer.

Ipso couldn't find a comfortable place to sit with his birth family. They were, for the most part, good, normal people of African descent who spent Sundays in church and work days working. They reveled in purchasing things with the money they earned; he was trying to make his way on slopes of wet rocks. There was one brother of his with whom Ipso could discuss the work of Miles Davis. But as soon as the conversation strayed, even to something as mild as how his brother's daughter was doing in school, the exchange became contentious.

Ipso's regular days, to say nothing of his work days, were fraught. Words would rush to the front of his brain in the factory and the work seemed two or three times more difficult than it should have been, or than it was, or than it was for the other people he worked with, or all three, which seemed a fourth possibility.

There were, to his mind, very few people who could do factory work and something else and do either thing well. There was a person back in the twentieth century who had made it to the Detroit City Council after attaining a law degree while working in the factory and, based on the interviews Ipso read, this person, Ken Cockrel Sr., had two brains. One brain coped with the factory while the other consumed law books. Ipso, on the other hand, was only able to string together a very few words and he left them in his mind, as they seemed to need to germinate.

> *Monkeys with torches and hand grenades riding pigs into hell*
> *seeking the enemy among them*
> *Monkeys with the reins between their teeth and the torches and*
> *grenades in either hand,*
> *Some with saddles some without,*
> *Some with letters from home attesting to bloodlines,*
> *Records that may be lost forever in the battle to come,*
> *And who will know which among them is the writer, the enemy,*
> *or one in the same?*

These words came to Ipso one stormy Monday night and festered in him deep into Saturday sleep. He tossed and turned, rolled and tumbled, wondering how to make things fit, how to get those pigs into the narrowing space. How could the monkeys be the riders, as pigs were probably smarter than monkeys and therefore would have to be the riders, even though the idea of pigs riding monkeys was laden with logistical challenges? The riders would have to be chimpanzees or at least carnivorous humans. Ipso was a carnivore himself and admired vegetarians. There were a few vegetarians in the factory, and they seemed calmer and listened to the news on stations where everyone seemed calm and smart. He thought vegetarians were smarter than he was and he so wanted to be smarter than he was.

All the great writers from Harriet Tubman to Katherine Dunham, from Charles Burnett to Fannie Lou Hamer had all been smarter than he was or seemed so at the very least. Their work rose to the high stage where it could work the brain stems, spinal cords, respiratory and nervous systems of large numbers of people, came down like invisible rain to be carried by media irrigation systems to the dry places until there were few towns where their work hadn't bloomed, fewer still where some derivation of their plants had not sprung up. People ate them without knowing where they came from and their bodies didn't care and the children they birthed with the nourishment that fused the egg and seed didn't care. Some reached back to find the source of what they had eaten and drew richness from the journey even if they had died before finding the root of the root. Others just grew.

3. Take Shape

One Tuesday (which seemed just as bad as any Monday, though Wednesdays were worse and Thursdays were sad until they became Fridays when he walked, somewhat compensated, out of the factory, headed toward Saturday) he was wrestling with the monkey versus pig, round swine into narrowing orifice conundrums, and noticed a stirring in himself. He seemed slightly heavier than normal and a bowel movement was no relief on that score. Then a shape poked out of his abdomen. It didn't really hurt but he didn't like it. It was a dream injury. In the plain light of day, the thing stretched his skin so much it should have hurt and so he anticipated pain which was recorded somewhere but mostly in the places where he knew fear. The more he struggled with primates and swine, the more the pokes disturbed him and his sleep.

One afternoon in the plant, he was too drowsy to notice the Optical Touch Card Ancillary Firsthand (or OTCAF)

Scrapper was in the descent mode pre-widgetization. His hand was still holding the Meid on lock. He would have lost that hand to the two-ton scrapper except that a fellow worker (not surprisingly, a vegetarian) noticed the green and pink skull and cross bones warning signs flashing on the floor beneath the machinery and pulled Ipso's hand away just in time.

The incident shook him awake and, indeed, it shook him all night long. After that, he did all he could to ignore the shape of the thing that he now somehow realized was going to emerge from him. He took time off from the job. He tried to screen in his back porch. He loaded his cooler with beer and tried to purchase more Miles Davis from the 1964 to 1968 period only to discover he already had every single recording from that era.

He tried to spend more time with his family and friends. But the shape(s) kept protruding from him. When asked about this by startled friends and family, Ipso would begin talking about the weather or ask about the other person's work or he would ask if the person had been out of town recently, and if so, how had the weather been there, if the people in the city that had been visited spoke of unusual cloud patterns or noticed any prints in mud. If the person who had noticed the protrusions had not been away, Ipso would ask about the color of the houses or buildings on the street the person had taken to get to where the two of them currently sat or stood. Occasionally, the person would actually answer the questions. Some ignored the questions and asked Ipso what the hell was going on. Others would simply walk away quickly, traumatized. A few actually tried to talk Ipso through understanding what was going on inside of him. If these conversations didn't end with puzzled looks all around, they ended with Ipso frightened nearly to tears after probing the possibilities of what the thing might be. "Do you honestly expect me to figure this out while I'm on vacation?" he would scream, pound his fist on his knees, and then apologize for his outburst.

4. Birthin' No Babies

One Sunday night, the last day before he was to return to work, it dawned on him that the thing was about to emerge. Weeks ago, he had given up the idea of resisting figuring out who was riding whom and dealing with the size of the pigs versus the size of the hole. He had slept with the questions and awoke with the questions, a low grade fever, his pillow wet and his days spent staring at the trees in his backyard and listening to Tony Williams, Miles Davis's drummer, bang and fall silent on a recording called *Circle in the Round.* The drummer came and went, cymbals crashed like china to the rhythm, then fell silent and left a space that was less than an echo but more than an absence.

Ipso went to the Main Library on Woodward Avenue across from the Detroit Institute of Arts. He was torn when he arrived as he learned the Detroit Film Theatre inside the museum across the street had a Charles Burnett retrospective that he desperately wanted to see. But the fear of the thing in him emerging in the dark on an unsuspecting filmgoer (perhaps even a Miles Davis fan) gripped him and he walked dutifully to the library's main information desk.

"I am about to birth something," he announced to the woman behind the desk. This was not the standard response to her standard inquiry of "Can I help you?" especially from a male.

"The thing that is about to come out of me is somehow connected to words that have been in my head for a few days now. I am about to answer the question," Ipso continued.

The Main Library in Detroit is a rather august and classically stylish white marble building in the early Italian Renaissance style, with windows almost a story tall on the second level recessed into magnificent arches. Like many of the august things in Detroit, it was built near the early part of the twentieth century. August or no, the librarians were used to homeless people and or mentally ill people coming through the doors with inexhaustible queries. The woman behind the desk was somewhat new to her position, but assumed this was one such query, that is, until she noticed the shapes poking out of Ipso. She insisted he needed medical help. Ipso protested this vehemently. "It's the question coming to a head, can't you see?" he said and pounded his knees with his fists. He was about to pound his head when a long cylindrical thing poked out of him, formed an "S," a backward "S," a question mark, and fell back into him as quickly as it had emerged. He thought the woman's eyes couldn't have gotten any wider and that's when she called the ambulance.

The Emergency Medical Service was on the way and Ipso realized that he needed to talk his way into having this thing in the library. It had to be in the library or bringing it into the open would be even more difficult and dangerous. That was clear. He knew it as surely as he knew the question was nearly answered. He knew it the way Miles Davis and Miles's father (Miles Dewey Davis II) knew Miles had to be locked up on the family farm in East St. Louis to kick the heroin habit he had attained in New York searching for Charlie Parker before he discovered he could not write in the gregarious, Neo African, Jackson Pollock baroque voice of Charlie Parker even as he realized that Parker's polyphony arose from a deep and harrowing silence that was Africans talking openly amongst themselves about all they had seen since the Middle Passage, a well

Miles would have to tap in the dead black night. It was then Miles realized he had to work with more sculpted silence, that he was working with a heat so intense it needed to be shielded from the outside and vice versa.

5. Language Body

Days after Ipso had come to her, the Librarian began to have second thoughts about having sent him to the hospital rather than allowing what was in him to emerge in the library. It all started when she was contacted by a reporter who just happened to have been in the emergency room of Receiving Hospital when they brought Ipso in strapped to the gurney flailing and straining against his restraints almost as much as the shape, now clearly an elephant, was flailing and straining to get out.

While medical personnel were scrambling, it occurred to Ipso that he had to make a decision about exactly how this thing was going to get out of his body. The options seemed as limited as they were unappealing. One option made him think that he would never again complain about digital rectal exams. The other was through the mouth. This was, in some ways, even less appealing than the option he had ruled out, though, practically speaking, it seemed the less dangerous of the two.

Even in the microseconds it took Ipso to choose an orifice, another deeper part of him had moved the elephant toward his throat and tried to calm whatever muscles needed preparation to get the thing out. His rib cage began to expand, painfully at first, then relaxed to the point of unfeeling like a tooth disconnected from nerves in the flesh. The relaxation was in part a response to the awe he felt at seeing every story he'd ever read or heard pass before him like a bullet train. If Ipso had believed in ghosts, he would have seen one leaving. The train slowed and words came to him that seemed to have nothing to do with the answer to the primate/swine equations. He heard Rufus Thomas's song "Walking the Dog," but with different lyrics.

When the clouds fall to the ground
You will know where I can be found.
Trackin' crimes bigger than the sea
Can't see the forest strung up in a tree.
Stalkin' the fog,
I'm just a stalkin' the fog.
Emmett said ain't nothing to it.
He'll show you how to stalk the fog.

Ipso saw Rufus Thomas with a James Brown cape open wide like wings. Did it matter that Rufus wasn't a vegetarian or that he had never so much as entertained the idea? Not now, because the trunk of the elephant was out, smaller than Ipso would have thought and so shiny black it seemed silver in certain turns of the light.

The reporter told the Librarian that when the elephant had fully emerged, Ipso's blood drained from its skin as if washed by invisible rain. Besides being smaller than any other elephant, its tail was curlier, and the distance between its front and hind legs was greater. The elongation clearly facilitated what everyone assumed to be a message on its hide. If it was a message, it was not delivered with words. The markings may have been hybrid hieroglyphs. Someone suggested calling the Egyptologist who had helped to curate the exhibit at the Detroit Institute of Arts. Just before the call was made, a security guard walked over to ask Ipso about the meaning of the markings on the elephant's hide. Of course, it was too late.

6. Links to Great Works of the Past

No one ever confessed to posting the security camera video of Ipso pleading with the Librarian as the seemingly random shapes emerged from his body. She had stumbled upon the video online herself, searching for a long out-of-print book called *The Suburban Bitch*, about an African-American woman working as a domestic servant in the mid-late twentieth century, which of course meant the people she worked for were white. It seems the Librarian's grandmother had known the woman who wrote the book. It was written in prison as a part of the author's therapy, a way to work out the anger so clearly manifest in her crime. The story, virtually forgotten now, had made very serious headlines at the time, the same way the civil disturbances in Detroit in 1967 had made headlines and then been all but forgotten except as a touchstone for the city's decline.

What had really struck the nearly all-white jury, including the white foreman of the jury—elected foreman by the whites in the room because he had worked at Ford Motor Company as foreman and was thought to have the most experience with African Americans—was that the killing spree began and ended with the family pets.

The prosecutor had ended his opening and closing statements with references to the pets, how the former maid could have left them alone as they were unlikely to be called as witnesses, how the autopsy on the cat showed it had been slain first, before the people were killed, and how the dog's autopsy had shown it was the last victim. As it had been quoted in the paper, "This woman, who the family had trusted for years, effectively created a pet sandwich of death with the family as the mainstay and the corpses of the dogs and cats acting as the bread."

Among the things left out of most media stories was that the animals had been ritualistically slaughtered, while the people had been poisoned and slept into death, and that the family had been tied to chairs and sat waiting for the police at the dining room table, plates of exquisitely prepared food before them with a centerpiece of flowers on the table.

Later, in his blog, a graduate student, a playwright (was the name familiar to her?) in the combined disciplines of Art and American Studies referred to the murders as oddly paralleling and presaging some of the more extreme performance art. That reference had a link to the video of Ipso standing before the Librarian with a giant question mark popping out of his body.

The video surprised her on two accounts. First and foremost, she didn't realize the library had security cameras. Why had she never seen video of any of the other strange goings on at the library, like one of the library's biggest benefactors, who at every holiday festival would bring in her talking bird that recited the names of the US presidents in backwards order of their election or the homeless guy who only read two books: the dictionary and the city's ordinances, and would always have to be dragged from the building laughing hysterically? There were other odd recurring events in the building that had never been subject to an internet posting.

Second, who had posted the video? The security guards who monitored the cameras were the most obvious and therefore the least likely suspects. Why risk your job to post a video on the web? Then there was the site upon which it was shown, the site formerly known as I-Fuel, which had been bought by Unicorp and renamed U-Fuel. Being posted on such a well-known site would surely help it go viral.

The Librarian's mother called and asked if she had seen the video and was it the Librarian on the video. When the Librarian admitted yes to both questions, her mother became frantic. She wanted to know how the Librarian was going to cash in on the video. Why hadn't the Librarian called her to let her know what had been going on? And, finally, was Ipso in pain when the shapes emerged? The Librarian did not have answers to these questions when her mother asked them. Nor did she have answers when her boss asked virtually the same questions.

7. Wet Finger Seeks Breeze

The Librarian's boss did not want to continue to be the Librarian's boss. He wanted to be the mayor or someone who made more money, got on TV more often and ate at better restaurants. He was unsure how he would become the mayor or someone like her. He had been casting about for a campaign color for his yet-to-be-created yard signs, a bumper sticker slogan, a light or even a tunnel from which a light might emerge. The black shiny elephant on the shadowy video came to him like a bolt of illumination, a tailor-made antidote for the semi-shadow he barely admitted even to himself that he was floundering in.

When the Librarian's boss called her into his office and interrogated her, there was a woman in the room who seemed to her strikingly out of place. The Librarian could not tell if it was the woman's flowing clothes in browns, blues, and oh so cautiously muted reds and oranges, or if it was the white briefcase-like container next to the woman that made everything odd. The Librarian could not recall ever having seen a white briefcase, nor was she sure it was a briefcase as it seemed soft as cloth, but in fact was standing up like a briefcase and not like a cloth item which would have collapsed. The Librarian also thought about how the advent of portable computers had made briefcases all but obsolete.

About halfway through the conversation, the woman put her hand on the white briefcase as one would put a hand on a dog that needed calming. The hand all but floated down toward the metallic latches, undid them, and placed the case in the woman's lap. So the case must have been harder and lighter than it appeared. It wasn't until the Librarian's boss repeated himself that the Librarian realized the woman was moving slowly because she was focused on what the Librarian's boss was saying as the Librarian should have or could have been doing.

"Yes," the Librarian finally answered, "It was after the question mark emerged that I called the ambulance." The consultant wondered to herself how the Librarian or indeed anyone could tell the difference between the backward "S" and the question mark.

The audio on the surveillance video was always low, but the segment with Ipso was distorted as well. As the video was passed from viewer to viewer on the Internet, people began to speculate in the comments sections of various sites as to what Ipso was saying or if he was saying anything. Some began to supply their own words, some with music and some without. One person turned the grainy black-and-white video to sepia tone, slowed down the movement, and added the music from an old song:

> Glory glory, hallelujah, when I lay my burdens down
> Glory glory, hallelujah, when I lay my burdens down
> All of my troubles will be over, when I lay my burdens down
> All of my troubles will be over, when I lay my burdens down

One person added her own lyrics to be sung with voice alone:

it is deaf to color
blind to music
and holds them both
like atlas holds the world
only as he would be
for real
herniated
wishing for death
unable
to lay his burden down

Inevitably, someone added dialogue from an antacid commercial:

Feel like you swallowed something big enough to swallow you? Get rid of that beached whale feeling with . . .

"This video belongs to the Detroit Public Library, its patrons, and the Main Branch in particular. As Director, it is my duty to see to it that the video either becomes part of the Library's collection or that we put our own stamp on it by putting our stamp on the situation that created it, you with me on this one?" The boss nodded to the other two people in the room as if he were speaking to children or as if there were invisible rods connecting the other two heads to his own and the others would nod in unison with him if he moved just right.

The woman with the white briefcase nodded. The Librarian was perplexed. "How do we put a stamp on events that have transpired before so many eyes," she asked somewhat rhetorically.

"That's why I'm here," said the woman with the white briefcase.

"To birth another elephant?" asked the Librarian.

"I'm a consultant," the woman smiled, as something in the briefcase on her lap began to whirr softly.

8. Homework

The Girl had done as much of her math homework as she could tolerate and had gone over to the reading assignment. As best she could determine, the story was about a woman who had to tell stories or something bad would happen to her. It reminded her of the storyteller who used to come to her school. She thought about the long flowing clothing the woman wore and how she had all the stories memorized so she could look directly at her audience the whole time she was telling the story. The Girl sat in her favorite chair, closed her eyes, and tried to tell herself one of the storyteller's stories. She got as far as the part where two little girls had opened their door to a cold bear so that he could warm himself by the fire. That's when she was distracted by the noise from a television news story.

The Girl's father, per the instructions of the newscaster, had turned up the volume of the TV to hear the barely audible shriek of a woman who stood before a man whose body undulated in very strange ways. Then there was video of an elephant, though it was rather long for an elephant, its tail curlier and its skin blacker than black. It was so black no one had anything to which it could be compared. Nor could anyone determine the meaning of the writing on the side of the elephant, except for the Girl. The messages she saw were so clear to her that she assumed everyone else could decipher them as well. She was, though, so mesmerized by the sight of the elephant that she didn't hear the newscaster say that linguistic experts and code breakers from around the world had gathered to study what appeared to be a message on the elephant's hide because no one had any idea what the markings meant. She also didn't get the hints between the lines that the animal's health was in a slow but noticeable decline.

9. More Homework

The Librarian's boss had given her an assignment. She was to work with the media consultant to bring the elephant to the library. The goal was to turn public opinion towards demanding the elephant be brought to the place where Ipso had tried to have it. The Librarian was supposed to speak publicly, with firsthand knowledge, about Ipso's demands to birth the elephant at the library. They would run the audio of her "testimony" under the video of Ipso and his various body shapes. The Librarian's boss would then speak and intimate that the code on the elephant's hide might be broken and the message revealed, if the animal were to come back to the place its "author" had wanted it to be in the first place.

The media consultant was brought in with the anticipation of at least two obvious questions likely to arise once the scheme was made public. First, if the library thought it was such a great idea for the elephant to be there, why had they called the Emergency Medical Service to take Ipso away to the to the hospital? Second, if the library had some way of deciphering the code, why couldn't they just do it at the hospital?

10. More Homework Part 2

"Aren't you glad they don't have you all trying to figure out the elephant thing?" the Girl's father said to her as they drove to school. "You have a hard enough time with the school work they give you."

"I like the elephant," the Girl replied.

"Of course you do," her father snorted back. "That's probably why it's going to die."

At times like these, the thought of joining her mother would cross her mind. But that was as frightening as anything.

"I liked mama too," she said and turned her face to the window, and thought without speaking—*and I still like the elephant.*

Rides to school used to be among the best times in her life. That was when her mother was still alive. The Girl and father drove to school and listened to music her father had chosen just for her. If there were long instrumental passages, he would tell the Girl how her mother had found him working in the factory, how he thought he'd be there his whole life doing the things outside of the factory that made coming to the factory inevitable. Then one day, a man who worked at the factory who was neither a good hunter nor a good factory worker came to the factory to hunt.

The worker who could not hunt worked in a spot with a window just above his head and behind him. Birds nested there. He could hear them rustling and flapping against the window. Even when he resisted turning around, he was distracted. His distraction caused problems. Once another man further up the line almost lost a hand because the man who was not a good hunter or worker became distracted, forgot which button gets pushed before which lever. He was often suspended without pay. So he would go hunting to get more food.

Of course, when he reached the woods, he was overtaken by the sun in the trees, the birds in the trees, the sun on the grass, which trees grew near which rivers, the sound and sight of running water. One day in the woods, he was trying to remember if the gun he'd brought was for shooting birds or deer. Both were within range. He got a phone call from his wife with good and bad news. The factory people had mailed him a letter. He would never have to worry about being distracted in the factory again. He thought for a moment about staying in the woods. Then he decided that whatever gun he had brought would work fine on humans. He jumped into his car, drove to the factory, and began shooting.

Many people died and the shooter made himself the last among them. The man who was not yet the Girl's father was shifted to a different part of the factory while police gathered evidence in the area where he normally worked. That didn't take as long as removing the blood stains.

In the meantime, he refused to speak to anyone about it except those who had witnessed it with him. Then he noticed some of those folks drinking and taking other drugs more and more. Two of them became unable to leave their houses. Some couldn't walk through the gate. One person committed suicide. The people who owned the factory were besieged by reporters and referred the media to the people hired to help the workers cope with the killings.

One of those people was a dark woman with dark red hair. The man who was not yet the Girl's father was scheduled to talk to this woman about what had happened, about the fire from the gun that came through the night into his sleep. Whenever he came to a flight of stairs with other people around, he had to fight himself not to push them out of the way and run. He heard screaming when there was no screaming. He was losing weight, showing less and less interest in food, even though, now, the factory owners had made sure there was food laid out all over the factory.

On their first visit, the dark red woman brought tea which he did not drink. This was always where he would end the story when he told it to his daughter. He didn't tell the Girl that, though at first he wouldn't drink the tea, he was comforted by the fruity smell, jasmine. The woman always reminded him of it. His talks with her were the first and only times he ever reassessed his family, the first time he was able to empathize with his brother.

"Did you get a good look at his hands?" the woman asked him. Then she would wait. No one had ever really waited for him to answer. He began to take comfort from silence.

She liked him from the start and had to check herself that she didn't cross the boundary from professional therapist to romantic interest. But this was futile. He was the most honest person she had ever met, the most transparent patient. Her mind drifted to what he would be like in the throes of passion. She had never imagined that the patient that presented the least challenge she had ever had would be one with whom she would fall in love. She let their sessions run over time. She began bringing recordings of Miles Davis's first great band with Coltrane, Adderley, Evans, and Jones. It helped him open up about his relationship with his brother. She would touch his knee when she reflected upon something significant he had said.

"So, you actually liked the unsliced bread. It was the blood in it that didn't play so well," she had said during one of the breakthrough sessions. During the last of their scheduled meetings, she brought him flowers and held his hand, clearly steps over the line. He was stunned. He had been trying to figure out a good way to meet her outside of the factory-authorized therapy sessions. This seemed like a good opportunity to ask about that and so it was.

As it happened, he was an amazing and intuitive cook. Before marriage he had always gone out to eat (remnants of the bloody bread episodes, perhaps). But their new house seemed like a new world and he began exploring cookbooks, only to leave them behind after a few months, creating his own concoctions that were at least as good as what he had found in the books. When their daughter was born, he learned to prepare food for infants, toddlers, then pre-teens. The lunches the Girl took to school were the envy of all her classmates. She began asking her father for larger and larger quantities as it gave her joy to share what she had.

She had fond memories of her father joyously puttering around the kitchen, especially on Saturdays, while her mother sang along with opera on the radio, making fun of the bass parts she could never hope to reach. If there was an opera being broadcast that they didn't especially like, her mother would put on *La Traviata*. She wouldn't start the recording at the beginning. "The overture is wonderful, but too sad to start," she would say. "Let's go to the drinking song." And so, the father would have to take a break from cooking and waltz around the house with the mother to *Libiamo ne' lieti calici*.

11. More Is Less

His wife, like many of African descent that lived in her country, loved barbecued ribs, one of the hand-me-downs from their ancestors' southern slavery experience. The husband developed an astonishing rib sauce. People came from miles around to try it. He was on the verge of starting a business with it (Astonishing Rib Sauce or ARS as it came be known) when she became ill.

The doctor told her no more greasy barbecued ribs with the Astonishing Rib Sauce, no more red meat, but especially no more pork. Baked chicken and broiled fish were okay on the odd occasion. She didn't heed the warnings and insisted that her husband continue cooking pork ribs. He did so reluctantly but reveled in the joy she took from eating pork.

One day, though, he found himself at her bedside surrounded by weeping relatives. She had been allowed to come home because there was nothing doctors could do for her. The Girl recalled the scene with a double sadness: the change in her father and the loss of her mother, the inspiration for Saturday waltzes, the singer of songs.

For his part, it was as if all the intervening years of recovery and happiness had suddenly collapsed beneath him like a broken chair. He was back to the day of the killing spree. Nightmares crept forward and sleep waned. He felt as if he'd had no right to normalcy, to say nothing of joy. The murders and suicide became his sun and moon.

He posted the ARS recipe online along with his business plan. Opera was banned from the house. He did not consciously stop eating meat. It just happened. He never spoke openly about becoming a vegetarian, even to those who had witnessed the murders with him, though; they were the only people with whom he exchanged anything but pleasantries. He took no joy in it, but his cooking was as good as ever. He lost weight and spoke to his relatives less often, especially his brother.

As his relatives abandoned him, only his daughter, the Girl, was left to witness his decline. He tolerated her for a time, even comforted her as they grieved together. But, as she began to take solace in memories of her mother, he resented her recovery and resented that he could not dismiss her as he dismissed those who had not been traumatized and therefore, in his mind, could not understand. She had sunk to the bottom and managed to rise again seemingly on her own, and that was as far beyond his understanding as the markings on the elephant.

12. His Favorite Poem

The Egyptologist who worked at the Art Institute began to notice a shift in the calls he was getting. When the elephant first emerged, reporters took him to lunch in restaurants he could not afford. In a couple of cases, he was unaware of their very existence even though he had been in Detroit for years. But now, people were sending him notes that questioned his expertise and professionalism. Many of these letters came with copies of Ishmael Reed's "I Am a Cowboy in the Boat of Ra." Sometimes, they would send the poem alone. Soon he stopped opening letters, especially those with no return address.

13. Who Wants to Know?

One reporter who wrote for a weekly media outlet addressed directly to people of African descent had seen his ancient-looking great-grandmother that hardly ever spoke perk up when the elephant hit the media. In fact, when she saw the elephant on TV she became downright agitated. After a few days, she stopped wearing her wig, and spent more time outside asking young people in particular questions that, in their minds, confirmed her as mentally ill, questions like: "What do you wear in the dark when you wear the dark?" "When was the last time you read something you wrote and heard another voice that was also your own?"

Years ago, she'd been buoyed but not overjoyed by the election of the first black US president. Though she did have tears over a slow smile when she heard him speak at his inauguration and say, "I know all this isn't for me." But the arrival of the elephant was different. She did not smile. She could not take her rest.

Her great-grandson, the reporter, had noticed the change in her. He sat down with her on different occasions to find out why she was so agitated. She would only repeat the questions she asked people from her front porch. While other members of the family thought she was becoming senile, the reporter saw something in her eyes and face that belied senility: the way she turned her head and nodded as she cut her eyes and smirked. There was the very slight but sardonic chuckle that made her body rock very slightly.

One day, his persistent questioning seemed to have paid off. Though the smirk and chuckle were still there, she said something out of the ordinary.

"Your friend doesn't know his trip," she said.

The reporter was so startled it took him a moment to ask what friend and what trip was she talking about.

"He can't read the elephant, can he?" she replied.

He guessed she was talking about the Egyptologist.

"Why do you call him my friend," the nephew replied.

"He thinks he should know how to read it and he doesn't know why he doesn't know," she said.

"About the elephant, you mean?"

"No, about the whale hiding in the toilet. Yes, the elephant!"

"But he's not my friend. I don't know . . ."

"You want to know. You think you should know. You don't know why you don't know. That makes you and him friends.

Only, he can mess things up and you can only tell people how he messed up after the mess, which is amazing considering that's what you get paid to do."

This is when the reporter decided to contact the Egyptologist.

14. What You Eat

The Librarian and the media consultant sat together in a room with the white device that looked like a briefcase. It whirred.

"The sample please," said the consultant.

The Librarian handed her a small electronic storage device on which the Librarian had placed her dissertation. The consultant began to transfer the dissertation from the device to the machine and to read it during the transfer. She was surprised in part because she had expected a smaller sample and also because of the content.

"I thought you were a librarian."

"I obviously am a librarian or we wouldn't be having this conversation, would we?"

"Usually people's graduate work has some semblance of relevance to their chosen profession."

"I was hired to run the Media and Public Relations Department. Then I was the department. Then the department was eliminated. Things happen like that. You get backed down or into something you never imagined and then you're stuck."

"Or, you get what you deserve."

The Librarian chuckled and said, "I know it's our fault we were tossed from the garden we never made." Then she stopped laughing abruptly and said, "Let's get on with it."

The consultant continued feeding the dissertation into the device. She could not help but read it even though much of it seemed incomprehensible. As best the consultant could make out, the Librarian proposed a link between the US cultural take on original sin and the growing fascination with and diversity of fried foods, drawing a parallel between how Carnival and Lent necessitated one another and provided the basic fuel for cable television.

People had come to batter and fry all manner of sweet and savory foods from candy bars to beer. But the big breakthrough had come when a scientist in a lab funded by a very large and relatively new church discovered a way to soften metal and other inorganic materials with a chemical that bonded particularly well with a patented mixture of sugar, salt, and genetically modified lard. Now segments of the population were frying and eating whatever was not poisonous. This included nails, bits of used tires, cassette tapes, coins, old toys, keys, the tops to coffee mugs that no longer fit, mismatched socks, earphones, the name tags and leashes of dead pets, floppy discs, bobble-headed Elvis statues, and pre-digital identification cards.

Certain congregants of the church that funded the new chemical for frying were reenacting their wedding ceremonies and chemically treating, frying, and eating their wedding rings as a way to internalize their commitment to one another. They did this with little or no consideration for the ultimate fate of consumed objects that couldn't be absorbed by the body, unlike those who fried and ate their mortgages and reveled in the items' transformation.

"Why did you bring a dissertation and not letters or something smaller for the machine to read?"

"My boss insisted upon the dissertation. He's friends with folks who were on my committee at school."

With that, the consultant rolled her eyes and said, "Oh, of course, the committee." After a few moments, the machine produced a sample script. The consultant handed it to the Librarian, who examined it.

"This is pretty simplistic," said the Librarian without looking up from the paper.

"It's designed to sound like you," the consultant said with a sugary smile that she let fall immediately.

"Then I could have written this by myself."

The consultant smiled again and said, "Well then, you should be able to record this in one take and we can both be on our respective ways."

15. Keep Hope Alive

There were many things the little Girl liked about the elephant. Its color was amazing. She had never seen anything so black. At one point, she wished the pages of her books were that black so that she might be able to read everything as easily as she read the symbols on the elephant's skin. Then she realized the reason the symbols on the animal were easy to read was not so much because of the blackness but because of the lustrous sheen that contrasted with the blackness and was made possible by the blackness, the silver that gave the symbols their knife's edge clarity. Then there was the message itself, how it seemed to speak directly to her even though she was sure everyone could read it, had read it, and was as comforted by it as she. The very simple message was so powerful because it came from an unknown source but spoke directly to her needs. Someone, something she had never encountered, had by purest chance made a place for her where before there had been no place or virtually no place.

She was perhaps most comforted by the thought that things could have gone the other way. It was as if she could see to the bottom of the ocean, the ocean that cared for her not one whit yet could not help but to reveal glowing fish of indescribable hues, plants that shimmered and waved, and wrecks made anonymous by new life, all of which the sea had made possible.

There could have been another message or no message at all. The man could have died instead of divulging the elephant. The elephant could have come with illegible markings or no markings. There could have been nothing there for her and she could have still found comfort because the message had changed nothing but her attitude. It was as if she had just discovered that the sun shines when there are clouds, shines when your part of the world has turned for relief to night, and shines when you die. Her mother was gone and the star that held the earth in orbit still burned.

16. The Committee on Dark Revenue

It was the guards who began to notice the elephant was dying or at least were the first to take the situation seriously. They had all won lotteries to take the job of guarding the elephant in the hospital. Everyone thought their jobs would be more glamorous than they were if not easier than they seemed. When they had won their positions, most of their coworkers at the agency slapped them on the back, hugged them and wished them well.

The real trouble started when reporters began to swarm around the hospital until administrators had to call editors and publishers and, ironically, threaten the media outlets with bad publicity if the reporters kept crowding the emergency room and parking areas where ambulances should have been. Every janitor and surgeon was recorded giving his or her take on the meaning of the markings on the elephant. For a moment, each interviewee seemed to take on some of the silvery blackness of the puzzling symbols on the hide.

Of course, the guards spent a great deal of time simply staring at the elephant. They began to notice how the wrinkles in its skin were becoming slightly deeper, day by day. They only spoke of it amongst themselves, at first because they assumed others would notice it and they didn't feel it was up to them to go beyond their job description. They were hired to keep the elephant from harm from the outside. They couldn't tell what brought on the changes. They also assumed other people were paying such close attention that surely someone would note the changes in the elephant's skin.

In the meantime, it gave them what seemed like secret knowledge because they spoke openly, at least amongst themselves, about something no one else mentioned. It seemed that it took others longer to realize the change in the elephant's skin, and even when those outside of their circle noticed it, they refused to acknowledge it openly.

At the height of the media attention, the deepening of the skin folds was evident even to the casual observer. But it took the obscuring of the symbols to spark public acknowledgement that something was very wrong, though that acknowledgement was not nearly as intense as the drive to understand the symbols. The shiny blackness became less black and less shiny and, for the first time, the elephant began to make noise.

The sound was surprisingly deep for a creature that was no more than four feet tall. It was voluminous. It could have come from a creature as big as the building. You could hear nothing but the sound when the elephant raised its trunk into an "S" shape and bellowed. The PA system near her in the emergency department could not be heard when she let loose. It was clearly a sound of distress and despair, but as large and overwhelming as it was, some thought they could discern finer, more nuanced emotions and messages from the sound. Those who dreamt about it were afraid to speak of it in the light. Just as the questions from the media previously had seemed to bathe the interviewees in glory, discussion of the sound brought something no one wanted to mention. "What do you think it means?" someone would ask. The response was often a shake of the head and a look towards the floor.

Veterinarians and zoologists that specialized in pachyderms were flown in, and they asked that the elephant be kept quiet, that the reporters and cameras be moved away. They were moved for a few days. The animal began to perk up. Though it stopped bellowing, the folds didn't reverse.

But after about a week of no media coverage, people began to call reporters and media outlets to ask what was going on. The hospital legal team got an injunction to keep reporters, videographers, and other photographers away. Soon, people began to show up at the hospital. Cars circled the parking lot like vultures. People fought over the spaces. Patients and their families were being outnumbered in the lobbies and other waiting areas. Everyone wanted to glimpse the elephant. Everyone wanted to cast off the pall that came when the animal's true condition arose in conversation. Everyone talked about deciphering the symbols. But the few who managed to struggle into the inner sanctum to actually see the animal just stared, surprised at how small it was, how the black they saw was not the black they had seen on television and other video, but was still blacker than anything they had seen or imagined. When spectators remarked on the color, the guards would close their eyes to recall the elephant's color when they had first been brought in to guard it. Every once in a while a guard would bend down to talk to a curious child and say, "I wish you could have seen it."

17. You Ain't Heard Nothing Yet

Cameras had been banned but, eventually, someone snuck one into the viewing area, recorded video of the elephant, and posted it online. It was too much for the rest of the media, especially the TV stations. A judge granted a court order that prohibited the hospital from keeping the media out. The cameras returned and the elephant's health began failing again. The "S" shaped trunk was raised and the deafening sound returned, this time with enough force to show up as visual noise in the live video transmissions. People covered their ears. Some wore the same protective ear coverings as airport ground crews. Nothing worked.

The last thing on most folks' minds was moving the elephant from the hospital as the Librarian's boss was planning, but he still pressed ahead. The Librarian and the media consultant completed their respective tasks of recording and packaging a message that said the best thing for the elephant was to have it moved to where its "author" had wanted it to be in the first place. The Librarian's boss held a news conference with the consultant and the Librarian. He showcased the recording of the Librarian even though she was there. He spoke about "the need to fulfill the wishes of the creator of the symbols so that then perhaps scholars will be able to discern their meaning."

This was the first time anyone had publically referred to Ipso as the "author." It set off a bit of a debate. Clearly, the elephant had emerged from him. But now that it was out, he was dead, and no one (except the Girl) could make heads or tails of the message. Was there a message? If no one could read the message, was Ipso an author? If there was a message, was Ipso *the* author?

18. The Media Consultant Was Born in Prison

The little Girl's father was shouting so much at the TV that she ran into the room. "They don't know what he was really like!"

"He who?" she asked.

"My brother, your sniveling uncle," the Girl's father replied. "His genes must have passed right through to you. You deserved him more than I ever did."

"Deserved what?"

"Do you know what it was like? He was always distracted. He concentrated so hard when he cut the unsliced loaves of bread that he cut himself, and I always got the bloody piece. Our parents insisted on buying uncut loaves. I ate bloody bread every day until I moved out."

"His hands must have been all scarred up."

"That's why the funeral had to be closed casket."

"Because of his hands?"

Her father rounded on her, teeth bared, as he all but spat, "You don't know what it was like."

She didn't reply. She had suddenly recognized one of the people on TV, the woman in the flowing dress.

Besides the elephant, the blackness of the elephant and the clarity of the silver, seeing the storyteller was the best thing about her life at the moment. It was also unbelievably wonderful that the storyteller was somehow involved with the elephant. The red-faced man with the perpetually moving lips spoke a comprehensible word or phrase now and again. He wanted to move the elephant, and every time he mentioned the idea, the storyteller would nod. The woman next to the storyteller didn't seem as connected to the event that was taking place, while the storyteller was brimming like the man who couldn't stop moving his lips and whose tongue occasionally came into view. This other woman was looking around as though she wanted to keep the looking around a secret. The Girl could feel her making notes.

The storyteller seemed a bit like the elephant because there were two parts to her color, at least two parts. Clearly she was dark and light, not as dark as the woman making notes, not as light as the red-faced man. But the real joy was that the storyteller and the elephant were somehow connected, that the storyteller, at least according to the red-faced man with lips in constant motion, was helping to save the elephant.

It is so good that I am awake and not dreaming, the Girl thought.

The Librarian's boss's campaign to move the elephant to the library hit some snags. None of the people with veterinary experience supported the animal being moved. He needed an ally, and while he tried to finagle connections and support on the medical front, he sent the Librarian over to talk to the Egyptologist. It just so happened that the reporter was also there. Juggling these two requests for his time reminded the Egyptologist of the days just after the elephant had emerged, days with more kineticism and exquisite meals than he'd ever known. It was the reporter, hoping to make the interview a twofer, who insisted that the Librarian, who had identified herself as such to the administrative assistant, be allowed to remain present during the interview. The Egyptologist, hungry for what he assumed would be good publicity, agreed.

"If you felt that you were close to discerning the meaning of the symbols, why did you quit?" the reporter asked.

"We didn't really quit," the Egyptologist replied, hoping the tenor of the questions would change.

"We?"

"My colleagues and I."

"Oh yes, your colleagues. I thought you said they were no help."

"Well, you need help on a project of this scale."

"Would you mind," the Librarian interrupted, "if I take a look at this book?"

She had been casting her eyes about, noting all of the unusual titles on Egypt and the Middle East when she stumbled upon *The Suburban Bitch*. The Egyptologist was silent. The Librarian had opened the book and read a few sentences before she realized he hadn't answered. She looked up to see him staring at the book with a look of embarrassment and fear.

"I'm sorry," she said, "I can put it back."

"My brother . . ."

"Did your brother write it?" the reporter asked.

"My brother's murderer wrote it and then she killed herself. I can't bring myself to throw it away."

19. Tell a Story, Win a Prize

"You realize," the teacher replied to the Girl, "that ours is not the only class to ask to visit the elephant and that there are many adults, parents and school staff, that have concerns about such a visit?"

"What if we just write letters that ask about moving the elephant? We could just say we want the elephant moved for all the reasons the people in the library say they want it moved."

"What are those reasons?"

The Girl had to think for a moment. She had not discerned the reasons put forward because she had been so enraptured by the sight of the storyteller. She also assumed that the teacher had seen the library people on television and actually knew what the man's lips were saying, assuming they had stopped long enough to create a sentence. The Girl's silence brought a sad smile to the teacher's lips. The Girl closed her eyes and said the first thing that came to her.

"I feel like this is the right thing to do."

She opened her eyes and saw the teacher's smile wasn't quite so filled with pity as it had just been, and it gave her confidence to press the issue.

"What if we just do it as a writing lesson, to practice how to write a good essay? We could make it an essay instead of a letter. We don't have to show it to anybody. It will still be good writing."

"Why does that make me dark," snapped the media consultant, looking at the skin on her bare arm as if to make sure it was still there. "And what does it matter?"

"Well you're right of course. You can say you are lighter or darker—that's your choice—or be between the two."

The Librarian tried to be as nonjudgmental as she could. She spoke in her best "can I help you voice," mustering the kind of sincerity she reserved for children, the elderly, or those who came to the library to practice their English. She waited a moment before sitting next to the consultant. She waited even longer before she spoke again.

"I didn't know your mother was an author and I was sad to learn how she died."

Now the consultant felt a mixture of relief and fear, relief that the Librarian probably knew the whole story and would not probe her for details, fear that, despite her calm tone, the other woman might somehow use the information against her. So she tried to head the Librarian off at the pass and jumped to the facts that brought her the most shame.

"I can't help where I was born."

"None of us can. I wouldn't hold anything like that against you. I think you have overcome tremendous odds."

"A credit to whichever race I claim at any given moment."

"I am curious though as to how—"

"How I ended up as a media consultant? I dealt with everything pretty well until after the suicide. She had everything to live for. It was the book. They were talking about changing her sentence to time served. I thought, this is it. The long funky nightmare is coming to an end.

"Then one day, about a year ago, I was visiting a school, doing my gig with a bunch of fifth graders. They had all heard the stories I had to tell before I arrived. I didn't care. I was good and I had my stories here and here," she pointed to her head and heart as she spoke. "I looked straight into their eyes. It works every time. You can stop a snake in mid-strike or a charging bull if you catch the eyes the right way. I learned that from the storyteller that used to visit the prison. She looked like she was a thousand years old, clearly dark, had a way of laughing to herself and the cutest impish smirk. Anyway, I had done "Snow White and Rose Red" and I was pretty far into Scheherazade when someone called the teacher to the door. Then the teacher called me. It took her a while to get it out, that my mother had hung herself with a sheet. I haven't told a story since that day."

***

It took a few days for the Girl's class to write the essays in support of the elephant being moved to the library. Most of the essays weren't very good. Most of the students thought the elephant was strange and they didn't really understand what the fuss was about. The Girl was one of the few that took the writing assignment seriously.

I believe the people I saw on television talking about moving the elephant to the library had the right idea. I believe the man that gave birth to the elephant would have been thanked by all of us if he had stayed alive. He would have been thanked for putting such a joyous message into the world. Now that he has said all there is to say about color, about how we see the two colors, black and silver, we can all solve many, many problems. We should be thankful for his ideas or perhaps just use his ideas since he probably wanted us to use them and has no use for them now.

I am sure, when we stop to think about it, we will all agree that the library is the place where people go when they want a better way to see the world, not the hospital.

The teacher had to point out to the Girl that her first draft didn't actually explain the message.

*** *

Upon their arrival, the Librarian's boss couldn't focus on anything except the students' essays. The Librarian was overcome by what she had learned about the media consultant.

"It's a mind boggling story, really. Her mother was in denial about the pregnancy, the assault, everything but the murder."

"We could sponsor a contest, her boss pronounced, oblivious to what she'd said. 'Give us your best elephant story.' What would be an appropriate prize though?"

"They wouldn't even let her out to have the baby. Then, years later, when they might have let her out, she kills herself."

"This is the essay we'll use. Let's call it a letter. Listen to this, 'the library is the place to go when you want a better world.' I wish I'd had this at the news conference, but no matter. I have it now and the world will have it soon, and they won't be able to resist it."

"She had told the 'Snow White and Rose Red' story hundreds of times and never focused on the lines 'Snow White, Rose Red, will you beat your lover dead?' It had just washed over her without sinking in."

"I won't need the consultant this time. We'll get the student to read on camera."

"And then there's the switch from storytelling to media consultant after memorizing virtually the whole fairytale canon so she could recite them without text."

"But we may need her to help guide the children."

"I don't think she really needs to probe the whole career switch thing, the trauma behind it."

"I need you to get the consultant on the phone."

"She split."

"What?"

"She and your pal the Egyptologist, who, as it turns out, is her uncle, they just split, went off. I don't know where. You could call the Art Institute and ask them where Egyptologists go when they go."

Days before the news conference, the teacher went to the library with more than a suspicion that no one had really read the Girl's essay. There wasn't even a hint of news about the message on the elephant's hide. That gave her some hope for success.

Once contacted by the Librarian's boss, the Girl's father had kept her out of school and given in to the plans to put the Girl on camera, despite pleas from the teacher who tried to dissuade him from both actions. She thought putting children in front of cameras was an especially bad idea. Among other things, she insisted children need privacy. But most of her ideas about how to treat children were ignored, even in the school where she worked. She thought perhaps if she could contact the Librarian, she might be able to persuade her to persuade her boss to read the essay himself, to take the glory and accomplish his goal to boot, though she feared the elephant might not make the trip from the hospital to the library.

When she finally arrived at the help desk, the teacher almost didn't recognize the Librarian as the person from the online video of the news conference. Her bright copper skin was nearly ashen. The eyes that had darted around at the news conference were still and aimed low.

"Hello there."

"Can I help you?"

"Actually, I am not in search of a book."

"Then this is strange place to be, isn't it?"

"The little Girl who wrote about the elephant being moved, I'm her teacher."

"You and everyone else in driving distance."

"I was hoping to persuade the gentleman I saw on TV not to . . . she's very young to be in front of so many people."

"But you would be the perfect messenger, right?"

"Actually, no, I think the gentleman—"

"That's no gentleman, that's my boss."

"—would be the best person to—"

"You got something against humor?"

With that the Librarian turned to face another patron walking toward the help desk. The teacher felt desperate. "Have you actually read the essay?"

The Librarian turned away from the patron and back to the teacher. Many had come claiming to be the Girl's teacher, mother, former dentist, or cousin who just happened to be in town for the taxidermists' convention. But none had asked that question.

20. Return of the Elephant Girl

Before the Girl's teacher came to the library, the Librarian's boss and the Girl's father had come to an agreement. As a result, the Girl had been spending more and more time with the Librarian in preparation for the news conference where the Girl would read her essay about why the elephant should be moved to the library. The Librarian was very nice, but the Girl couldn't help but wish the storyteller was there to help instead of the Librarian.

"She ran away?" the Girl asked.

"Sort of."

"Does her mother know?"

"Her mother's dead."

"Does her father know?"

"He's dead too."

"I know how she feels. How did her mother die?"

"It's a long story."

"I would love a long story like the storyteller used to tell."

The Librarian would have also loved a long story and she wanted to speak with the "storyteller" as well. She had come to see the media consultant in a new light. She could imagine them having coffee and conversation about feeling forced to change the ways they had earned their living. The Girl wanted to talk with the storyteller about how she had felt when her mother died.

She had been thinking about her mother more often. She drifted off while she and the Librarian were practicing answering questions about why the elephant should be moved or if he should be moved. Sometimes, she would hear a voice telling her the storyteller's stories. Sometimes it was the voice of the storyteller, but more and more often it was her mother's voice. Then her mother would stop telling the story and begin talking about what a wonderful time they had all had in the kitchen on Saturdays listening to the opera, smelling the food her father prepared, and dancing. Sometimes, the Girl would smile for what seemed like no reason to the Librarian. Sometimes, she would be on the verge of tears. The only thing the Librarian knew for sure was that on those occasions of joy, distance, and sorrow, the Girl had left the room the way readers leave a place for the book they are reading. The Librarian thought this was a bit curious because she had noticed the Girl actually had trouble reading, so much trouble that she had begun harboring doubts that the Girl had written the essay.

Strangely, her boss had not let the Librarian see the essay. She had taken his word that it supported the idea of the elephant being moved to the library. The Girl confirmed that much. But there was something unsettled about the Girl and the elephant or something unsettled in the Librarian's mind.

21. Theory Conspiracies

The elephant's guards had become very weary of reporters. They were pursued and interviewed on the job, in the parking lot, at the bus stop and at their homes. They were profiled to within inches of their very existence. At first, they consented because it was a chance to talk about the elephant. But their talk didn't help revive the elephant. It seems the drama of the elephant's prolonged agony made a better story than any potential recovery. They began quitting in small groups and reconvening at a bar several blocks north of the hospital where they didn't think most reporters would tread because reporters didn't know the place existed and, they thought, it was not the sort of place reporters were used to frequenting.

The place was called the Deep Seven. The regulars were unsure who owned it. Some thought it might be the cook, a white looking blond woman with a thick, phony German accent. Others assumed it was the bartender, who seemed like a darker version of the woman and said he was born around the corner though no one from the neighborhood ever recalled seeing him or his family in the area during the time he claimed to have been raised there.

It was a place with a lot of things that didn't exist in many other places anymore: payphones with rotary dials, ashtrays, bathroom stalls with small round windows, transoms, and a jukebox with vinyl records. That juke box was the attraction for some of the more adventurous students from the university several blocks away and for the reporter whose grandmother had inspired him to visit the Egyptologist.

Friends of the reporter had told him about a strange dive of a bar with Ellington and Brahms on the juke box. When he finally got around to visiting, he discovered Mingus, T-Bone Walker, and Copeland on the box as well. He put many coins in the machine and began playing Monk and Satie tunes back to back. The combination of music struck the bartender, who offered the reporter a free drink. This was noted positively by those who thought the bartender was also the owner.

"We're always glad to get students in here. We need fresh faces and blood, livens up the place, breaks the monotony."

"Actually I'm a reporter."

The bartender laughed. "My folks have had enough of the media for a while. This is one place they could escape. Reporters even followed some of them home. But they don't show up here for some reason. We began to think of this as an embassy."

"Who's being protected from what?"

The bartender took a moment to breathe deeply. On the one hand, the young reporter seemed like a trustworthy, square business sort. On the other hand, how could he not have recognized the patrons?

"So, Mr. Reporter," he said with a smile, "what's the latest on the pachyderm?"

Now the reporter felt like he was talking with his grandmother and he needed to fish for the right answer. With her, questions that seemed to come out of the blue were often connected to something bigger that was directly at hand but not always visible. The reporter's silence gave the bartender pause. I've let them down he thought. This guy is going to give a signal and the place will be crawling with cameras and mics in no time.

"It depends," the reporter replied, "on whether you're concerned with the message on its hide or its health."

"Is that an either-or proposition?"

"Am I unwelcome here because I have the wrong take on the elephant?"

"Who says you're not welcome?"

"Who's being protected from what?"

"There's a woman came in here days, weeks, or months ago with a machine. I thought I recognized her. She looked like a younger, lighter version of a woman who used to come in here all the time but years ago. The younger, lighter woman looked around the place like a . . . a surveyor, like somebody that had come back to a house they used to live in to see what the new folks had done to it. She had a machine with her, a white box. She was drinking heavy, depressed, I could tell. I cut her off. She was pissed but didn't leave. She noticed the juke box, walked over to it looking real sad. She waited for the songs on it to play out, asked for change, and started feeding it coins. She put about twenty quarters in it and played Dinah Washington till I thought I was going to die, two songs over and over: "Where Are You?" and "This Bitter Earth." I told her Dinah had lots of other tracks on there. Eventually, she pulls out her machine, starts fiddling with it and chuckling. I just thought she was drunk. The next day, I open the place up, go over to the box to put something on, and I start to feel strange, like I knew the machine or it knew me."

With that, the bartender handed him the drink.

22. The Digital Dog Ate My Paycheck

The Librarian's boss had been fiddling with the white machine the media consultant had left behind. At first, he loathed the machine because it reminded him of all the money he'd spent on the consultant that was now probably being spent with his erstwhile friend, the Egyptologist. Then he realized the consultant may have left notes or other materials that could prove useful and so opened the machine and began to try and figure out how it worked. It wasn't very intuitive. He screwed around with it for over an hour, forgetting that he had a meeting with the newly hired political consultant, who left increasingly angry voicemail messages. But the Librarian's boss had become entranced.

At one point he touched a pad on the machine that glowed. A fingerprint image, presumably his, appeared on the screen. Immediately after that, he discovered a program the consultant had never used. He knew it had gone unused because it triggered an initial setup screen. Even that was fascinating. The screen was accompanied by voices, velvety voices that reminded him of a girl from high school and a teacher he'd had a crush on. Stranger than that, the voices reminded him of the time he'd gone skydiving, the exhilaration and liberation he'd felt as he sailed through the air just before the chute opened, how he'd felt that he could do anything, having had death more than flash through his mind. It was at that moment the machine asked how it could help.

A vision came to him all but welded to his remembrance of the brush with death. It was hardly grand. But the flood of emotion and release was strong enough to make it grandiose. Suddenly, he had the crux of his mayoral campaign, and it was all in his hands. He didn't have to rely on a school girl's shallow plea to support the wishes of a man who, even when he was alive, wouldn't have been able to afford a good night out. The new plan would endear him to the people who could pay for his campaign and keep him in a manner to which he would love to become accustomed. Most beautifully, the pilot project could begin right there in the library.

23. Lost and Found

After the Girl's teacher had visited the library, the Librarian felt the same wave of doubt that had come over her when she had learned of Ipso's fate at the hospital. She went home and began drinking. When the phone rang, she answered with "Can I help you?" broke into tears and hung up. Seconds later, the phone rang again, and before she could say anything, the media consultant said, "Don't hang up!"

"Okay, okay, I'm sorry. I don't feel well. I'm surprised you—"

"We were each other's only connections. Once we started talking, our lives."

"I can't leave. I can't leave her there alone."

"What the hell! Is she locked in a tower or something? You're not her mother. You got to learn to—"

"Walk away from the problem like—"

"Actually the reason I called is that I need your help and you can only do it there. Hello, are you still there? Look, I am sorry. I know this may not be a good time to call but I stupidly left before I . . . you remember that machine?"

24. Dog Bytes Paycheck Part 2

The Librarian's boss was putting the machine through its paces, helping it find its voice, his voice, the voice that would propel him to nights out in the finer establishments:

"Can I help you?"

"If pandering means following the will of people even when it leads to tough decisions, then I pander."

"It appears you were three days late returning a book within the last six months. What were the circumstances of your lapse?"

"Do you deny the source of your campaign contributions make you beholden to a certain constituency with views outside of the mainstream?"

"The restrooms are currently at capacity. Your toddler must simply be patient until after our janitorial staff can make the area more hygienic."

"I believe the voters are too angry to be misled."

"Based on our conversation, I suggest that you may need to take on an intermediate volume before you read the one you're requesting, a stepping stone as it were."

"While these services were offered in the past, I suggest you may want to find alternatives. Begin to build community with neighbors of like mind."

He pushed the "reframe" button.

"While these services were offered in the past, now is an excellent time to assert your personal responsibility and move these issues from the public to a more personalized sphere."

The next step would be to get it to write layoff notices. How hard could that be?

25. And Your Mama Too!

"You don't seem to realize how her death affected you."

"Do you want your boss's print on the machine? Do you really want to see his mind manifest in digital form?"

"I saw his mind manifest every day at work. Why didn't you take the machine to the elephant?"

"Because, it's an elephant! It's not like it missed a step on the ladder; it's a whole other species, no prints, very little in the way of social memories and no language we can discern, huge feet instead of hands and an olfactory sense that probably overwhelms most of its cognitive ability. In short, it's an elephant!"

"She really misses you."

"The elephant?"

"The Girl."

"All the time we've been talking and you're still drunk. Listen, you need to make an appointment to see him as soon as possible. Pretend you're interested in him; tell him you'll help him pimp out the mayor's campaign—"

"He's working for the mayor?"

"He wants to run for mayor and the machine might help him."

"Don't you feel a void without her?"

"The Girl?"

"No, your mother."

The consultant was about to hang up. But then she had visions of the Librarian's boss ascending to ever higher office, his lips pausing only long enough to kiss the machine in private rooms. As she searched desperately for the right words, the Librarian broke the silence.

"If you knew what the machine was capable of, why didn't you use it for something good?"

"I'm not sure what it can do. I just have a bad feeling about programs I didn't open."

"You don't know the programs on your own machine?"

"Technically speaking, it isn't mine."

26. Waiting in the Sitting Room and Vice Versa

The Librarian and the Girl had come to see the Librarian's boss to confirm preparation for the news conference, which was scheduled for the next day. They had been waiting outside of his office for twenty minutes. The administrative assistant, who usually waved the Librarian through to the boss, had asked them to have a seat and notified the boss that the Girl and the Librarian were waiting. After that, the clock on her desk had her full attention.

Since the video with her and Ipso had been posted on the web, The Librarian had become used to not waiting so long to see the boss. In fact, she had often been ushered into his office with but a moment's notice and been given overwhelming tasks. Now she was worried. The waiting time had her worried and her agreement with the consultant had her worried. She had promised to retrieve the white machine in exchange for the consultant promising to see a therapist about how the loss of her mother had influenced her career change. The Librarian did not know if the consultant could be trusted to actually see a therapist and she had no idea what she was going to say to retrieve the machine.

The Girl was not worried. She had come to realize that what she knew about the elephant was not common knowledge, that the message that was so plain to her was indecipherable to everyone else. She had been overwhelmed when the Librarian had revealed that fact to her, but not overcome. She felt as if she had something of extreme value, that she had only to bide her time and reveal it at the right moment. She had, though, already composed an introduction to the message.

"Could you please read this?"

The Girl handed the Librarian a small piece of paper with handwriting:

I remember an old picture. Was I asleep? A woman clipped clean wet sheets to a thin line in the sun. People did not expect things to come so quickly. Did people dream of the wind that took the water from their clothes pinned to the line or did the scent of the sun in the sheets turn their sleep over and over? Black and silver one after the other, is this how the sun spoke at night, through the smell of its heat in a dream? Was I asleep?

"You wrote this?"

"I just handed it to you. It introduces the message. When are we going to be on television?"

"Who knows? Who cares? You wrote this? Your family didn't have a dryer?"

The Librarian began to feel a strange guilt that she had thought the Girl was barely literate. Then the Librarian became distracted. The administrative assistant's eyes lit up as the clock hit five o'clock. She stood to leave.

"I hope you have a good time on television," she said.

"When are we going to be on television?" the Girl said.

The Librarian had no reply. What's more, to her mind, there was no good answer except never. She hated being on television, in front of the media, especially with her boss. He never said anything she could support and he never stopped talking. She didn't especially like the more powerful, aggressive reporters either.

She had only become a media relations person because of an incident at college where she had been studying library science, a major into which she had also drifted. She had not declared a major, but a professor from religious studies whom she found both physically attractive and intimidating confided in her that he had once fallen in love with a librarian.

"Did you get to the library often?" she asked, then blushed at her own question.

"I think you'd do well behind the help desk," he replied, and she blushed again.

After that, she officially declared her major as library science, landing a work-study position in the psychology section of the library. Ironically, just as she was hired, the school fell on hard financial times and, with more students finding materials online, library staff was in serious danger of being cut.

That began to change when a graduate student, of whom she was vaguely aware outside of class, wrote a play, *The Official Report on Human Activity*. The text of the play got mixed reviews in the local media, but the fact that a play that was yet to be performed got any notice was a testament to the media relations skills of the playwright. He made five-by-five-foot posters with oversized text of quotes from the reviews, good, bad, and unintelligible, and plastered them illegally in strategic areas around town. Smaller text on the posters alluded to some of the more salacious parts of the play. The playwright granted the university library sole proprietorship over the text, effectively setting it loose in the public domain. The play was scheduled to be performed off campus thirty days after the posters went up.

The professor of religious studies had come to the library during the hours the Librarian was there, ostensibly to find his way through some lost books of the Bible. He approached the Librarian at her desk, oblivious to the line of students seeking her help. He was soon ushered to the rear where he waited a half hour to see her. He noticed all the computer terminals also had waiting lines. When his turn to speak to her finally arrived, the Librarian was frustrated and tired.

"The library has become quite the place. Are they serving beer somewhere?"

"If they are, I'll take two."

A group of three students rushed the desk.

"Excuse me, but we're looking for a copy of *The Report*," said their designated spokeswoman.

The Librarian looked up exasperated and handed her a form and a slip of paper with the number 244 on it.

"Take this number, complete this form, and return it to the next desk. Be sure to put your contact information next to the number from the slip. Any perceived alterations to the number will result in forfeiture of your position in the cue and you will have to begin the process from the start. Thank you and good luck."

With that the students walked away, staring at the information and forms.

"Is this play going to be performed—"

Before the professor could finish his question, another student approached the desk looking for a copy of *The Report*. The Librarian repeated the routine with the number and forms. The professor's curiosity was piqued. He lied to a security guard, who parted a line of students to allow him access to the text online.

The more he read it, the more upset he became. The play was about a young woman of indeterminate ethnicity who leaves her family to go fight in the brown hemisphere's water wars sparked by global warming, though it is unclear who she supports. Her grandfather is an old man who struggled with his career choice and only becomes disciplined enough to choose on his death bed. Her father is a banker who forces his most attractive clients to have sex with him but is plagued by nightmares.

In one recurring dream, he is a white woman in the nineteenth-century southern US, who, when it is discovered she is having sex with a half-dark house slave, is forced to escape with Harriet Tubman. Of course the house slave also has to vacate the premises.

The only thing that makes the trip even slightly bearable is that the woman and her lover are together. Though once, when they slip off to have sex, Tubman nearly leaves them behind to fend for themselves without map or weapon in the wilderness.

Right after that episode, the sky to the north darkens. That afternoon, it begins to rain. The party comes to a mountain as rocky as it is steep. Hounds bay in the distance behind them. The woman turns around to find Tubman and the escaped house slave arguing. His eyes that had always seemed soft to her are wild and tired looking. Tubman, on the other hand, is firm and fearsome. She flails her arms and points behind them, the direction from where they'd come. Then she stops. Her voice is low and calm.

"You trained the dogs, right?"

He shakes his head and looks around as if there was a path of escape just beyond his sight.

"Then it's settled. You go talk to the dogs before they get back to the slave catchers. Put 'em off our trail. Otherwise, we die trying to climb this mountain."

"What if the dogs don't act like they recognize me? What if they're too close to their masters right now?"

"Then we all die tryin to climb the mountain. I got one rifle and six shots left. I'd have to kill all of them with a couple shots. You think they gonna stand there, let me shoot 'em and reload?"

"Tell the truth, you want me to die. You hate me. Tell the truth."

"The problem with the truth is that there are all kinds of truth. There's the truth you can see, you know, dropped-rocks-fall sort of truth. There's the truth little children tell before grown folks get to 'em and teach 'em how to lie to get along. Then there's the unwelcomed, unclean, uglier-than-a-mule's-butt truth, and that's what's waiting on us right now."

The former house slave turns to his lover, his mouth open to shout but with no sound. He runs toward her, then past her.

The banker wakes up. It takes a moment for him to realize whose bed he's in. The sheets smell like the ones his mother used to pull off the line when he was younger, that she continued to pull off the line even after he'd bought her a state-of-the-art clothes dryer. (She had in fact refused to use many of the things he had given her even though she praised him sincerely for each and every gift. She wondered but could never ask what he remembered.) The sheets on the bed where he awoke smell like sun because the glass windows allow sun onto the bed. It is the home of one his clients. He can hear the ocean. He knows he is in California, but should not be close enough to the ocean to hear it. People are arguing, running up the stairs toward him. He hears a shotgun being cocked.

The religion professor did not read any further and remained perplexed as to the popularity of the text among the students. He missed the wilder hallucinations of the banker as he ran wounded from the client's home only to drown in the ocean that had made its way miles inland. He never saw the links to recipes for birth control and aphrodisiacs made from common clover and a particular circuit found in wide-screen televisions. He was completely focused on the slight relativity of truth to which Tubman had alluded, assessing the situations in the rain with the dogs behind and the mountain ahead. He decided not to attempt to ban the text but to expose it to the world (meaning the students' parents) so that they might ban it.

Though they tried to hide it with businesslike questions, the librarians were thoroughly upset when the professor threatened a campaign against the play if they didn't remove the text from the library (something they couldn't have done if they'd wanted). The play had made the library the place to be. The librarians had a gateway drug and they were using it to hook students to other writers, from Merce Cunningham and John Cage to the more traditional writers like James Joyce and Jimi

Hendrix. It was a dream come true. What's more, the increased traffic had at least delayed impending budget cuts and layoffs.

Even so, the religion professor informed the librarians that he believed that students were sent to the university to learn the truth, not to learn that the truth can shift based on circumstance, context, or perspective.

"Bringing pressure and light onto this work will give you a point of reference, an anchor from which you'll make better judgments when you are assisting the young minds that come to you for help," he told them.

The other librarians, who noticed the religion professor's fondness for their younger colleague, urged her to dissuade him from his campaign. One day she decided to try to engage him in a group discussion.

"Would you be willing to discuss this, perhaps with my colleagues and me?"

"Perhaps you and I should get together and lay the groundwork for the meeting. I know of an excellent restaurant. They know me there and would set aside a room for us."

She didn't blush as he expected. She had approached him with a rock in her gut. Before the arrival of *The Report*, mortgages, car payments, and college tuitions had been in the balance. The religion professor may have known that or he may have been as oblivious to it as he was to the line of students that preceded his turn in front of the Librarian. In either case, he appeared to her now in a strange unflattering light. She refused his offer with a lack of emotion that caused him to squint at her as if she had suddenly become difficult to see.

She managed to create a media campaign to inoculate the library and *The Report* against the religion professor's attack. The university hierarchy noticed a serious increase in inquiries and applications that seemed to coincide with the mailing of the *Ban Barriers, Not Books* brochure (though in truth, the increased interest was based on the play, which the Librarian had not read) and decided to promote the Librarian to Media and Public Relations.

Now, here she was, walking back to her office with a strange grade-schooler in tow after having been kept waiting for no apparent reason, having been effectively refused a meeting with her boss on the eve of a crucial news conference. On top of everything else, her distress over her demotions of the past few months began to feel like garbage she'd forgotten to take out. Back in her office, she tried to distract herself with a casual check of her e-mail and found a layoff notice from her boss, sent while she had been waiting outside his office. She called the Girl's father, told her to wait there in the office, and marched back up to the administrative area.

The Librarian's boss was about to send out his news release announcing that he would soon have an announcement (he intended to run for mayor and cut labor costs dramatically with "an ingenious new computer program to help and direct citizens that need help and direction without all the fussy human inconsistencies, moods, meal breaks or pay scales"); the consultant was just about to call a therapist; the Girl's father had finally arrived at the library to pick her up; the Girl had just added the last word to her revised essay (complete with her new treatise on the relationship of silver and black being more symbiotic than that of black and white, later to be cited as her first serious art theory text) in preparation for the next news conference (whenever that might be scheduled); and the Librarian had surprised herself by hefting a fairly heavy chair over her head in preparation for bashing down her erstwhile boss's door, when the news hit the media.

The Teacher, who didn't own a computer, had dusted off her television and was struggling with a distorted picture and no audio when she recognized the elephant's hide. There was video of the elephant's guards hugging each other and weeping along with some seemingly unrelated footage of a place called the Deep Seven. Someone placed a hand over the camera lens and it all went black.

The Whistling Dragon or Every Boy's First Murder

There's something supernatural about the way he walks.
There's something supernatural about the way he talks.
Coming from another world I know he doesn't find it easy
–Anthony Moore, "The Secret"

The Librarian

Don't get me wrong. I've never starved or been without shelter. I haven't done physical labor for pay since I stopped waiting tables. But you're reading this mostly because I've had desperate jobs; every one of them has turned into something that would never be on any job description unless you worked for the mafia or the CIA. In each case, the real description was unwritten and what was written described only a fraction of what was real or was an outright lie. Now, I know there are folks out there thinking that sounds cool. It's about as cool as going to a nice hotel and finding out you've checked in to a prison. It got to the point where I had to look up the history of the phrase "pig in a poke" because it was on a loop in my skull.

You would not think a degree in library science, especially coupled with a degree in mass communications, would lead to a desperate job. The thing is, I was better at media relations than library science and ended up with what I thought was a media job at a library. As many twists as there are to that story, it's fairy tale-simple compared to what happened afterward: assault charges, being sued for property damage, a bit of jail time, and then things got interesting.

***

When it comes to jobs, I have always admired Marx, Freud, and Einstein. Don't get me wrong. I am not really a Marxist and Marx had it pretty rough actually. Freud was a sexist pig and I am sketchy on the details of the general and specialized theories of relativity. I am not male, Jewish, German, or Austrian. What strikes me about what I call "The Big Three" is their unparalleled influence on the last century (the twentieth) and how that influence came strictly and utterly from what they wrote. It wasn't their money. They commanded no armies, held no public office. They published what they thought and set one whole century on its ear. I've decided that's the job for me. I am seriously revamping my resume.

So far, whenever someone's taken notice of me because of what I've written, I've ended up holding the bag, the poke with the above-mentioned pig. Even friends, people seriously in my corner, wound up leading me to what turned out to be a dark alley. It wasn't their fault. They weren't in control, and it's about control, trust me. This latest job I've lost sort of started with me trying to reduce my jail time. My only tools were my words and my library science. All things considered, I was relieved to be in an institution with virtually no physical violence and fairly professional staff. (I heard stories from inmates transferred from other facilities, tales that would put hair on your teeth, believe me.) But a relatively nice lock-up is still a lock-up.

The first thing I did was whip the library into shape. Staff told me the Dewey was too complicated for most inmates to follow. I actually used that to my advantage. I told folks the COs didn't think inmates were smart enough to check books out of the library like everyone else. Many didn't care, but, those that did raised enough of a stink to get the Dewey in place. Next, I needed people to work the desks. I decided to train folks with relatively little time to do. I pleaded with them to send news releases to the media when they got out. I wrote the releases. All they had to do was send them and answer the inquiries about the library with the training and verbiage I gave them: how they'd been "inspired to pursue library science as a career after incarceration" (whether they intended to or not). A couple of folks actually contacted the media. It worked. News crews were at the prison gates a few weeks after the first release went out.

I should explain something here. I don't like being on camera, in front of the mic, or even talking to print folks (in that order of most to least egregious). Ideally, I come up with the ideas that get other people publicity and stay out of the spot. But I had to bite the bullet on that one. PR for other people was not going to get me out. The only good thing about my reticence was that I didn't have to pretend not to want to be out front. You can check the YouTube clips (Books Behind Bars). I was not ready for prime time. My shaky, pale, deer-in-the-path-of-a-freight-train look belied the months of hard work I had put into getting my story out, but seriously added cache in terms of sincerity, not creating the library strictly for publicity, blah, blah, blah.

Even so, that wasn't enough to get me released. In fact, one inmate told me I would be inside at least six months for every day my victim spent in the hospital. I don't know where that formula came from but it didn't bode well. My erstwhile boss had spent four days in the hospital after the door fell on him. I asked the woman with the formula if follow-up doctor visits counted and she said she'd have to get back to me on that.

What the library story got me were privileges. The warden allowed me to create a library newsletter both print and online. The online version could be seen by people on the outside. That's how my friends, a former co-worker (of sorts) and her uncle, found me, and that's what they used to eventually get me the gig that helped reduce my time.

Ironically, I despised my ex-co-worker when I first met her. Things were rocky even after we became friends. But when she stepped through the door of that visiting room, when I saw light on a face I knew from the outside and I realized no one else had come to see me, my tears streamed. I was so focused on what I had lost; I didn't even realize my cheeks were wet until she told me. You just don't know.

***

The CEO

I thought I had given my unfortunate, would-be biographer the "slip" as they used to say, and the Deep Seven seemed like a chance to put the last nail in a coffin I was only too glad to see closed. I could now give up on my "story" to the extent that it was mine. It had collapsed from under me (something I had in common with the former owners of the DS), turned on me, become public and out of control.

I could have tried to invest the money I had left from my salary and, along with my options, had enough to live anonymously, that is to say alone. But that seemed a bleak fate and the Seven offered me a chance to keep my distance and to acquire friends as guests. The place would have to remain closed for a while and reopen with a new name and feel, but with no "under new management signs," no markers of the transition. One day it would simply be what it is now, "The Whistling Swan," and everyone would have to accept that or create his, her, or its own answers to the questions about how or why it had changed.

I don't know how much you know about so-called real estate transactions, but they can be nefarious deals, especially if you want to avoid being part of the public record, and there is little I wanted more than to avoid the public record. You must hire a lawyer. Is there anything stranger than having a stranger handle private details and information in order to guide you through a system that is anything but private? I have had to do that twice now, once to buy the building that became the Whistling Dragon, and the second time in a vain attempt to avoid Texas's rather active death row. In a way, I was lucky to be on the American continent and in the US, as the legal system here works fairly well. But, even in the US, it works better in some places than it does in others and better for some than it does for others. Had I not virtually run out of money (what I didn't pour into the Dragon went to bribes, leaving relatively little for legal), and had my first crime not been in a state with, as my biographer put it, "an ironic and noxious blend of the Puritanical and the reptilian," things may have been different.

Even so, as time goes on and the effects and affects of the experiment fade, I have become less and less bothered by the notion of death, that is to say, the human sense of legacy. The strange interplay of memory, nostalgia, and hope is leaving me. Once this is over, it is over. How a species that has been able to determine the age of the Earth, extend its lifespan, and send objects to the edges of the galaxy could fear death or regret the past—to say nothing of believing in things for which there is little or no evidence, God and the afterlife for example—will be a mystery long after I am dead, reverted, or both.

Of course, in terms of the afterlife, there was also the speculation of the Veiled Woman, yes, the very one that virtually closed the place with her arias and Bible-burning song. She'd walked into the venue a "true believer" in the aforementioned peculiarly strict form of Christianity that hails from the south. After some time though, she imagined that the afterlife may be as mysterious to "us" as this life is to a creature in the womb, that just as there is no way to convey to even the brightest fetus the complexity and enormity of the natural world or human society, what awaits humans at the other edge of life may be equally beyond our grasp.

Speculation has become one of my principle pastimes here on death row. I have tried to imagine what would have happened if my desire to be with people, albeit at a certain distance, had faded from me before the Deep Seven went up for sale. I probably would have invested my money and lived until I disappeared. My appetites would have changed. I may have avoided the light (I am writing this now with lights out, surely a residual of the old form) and probably would have been discovered one day by a surprised accountant or servant (would I have hired people to "keep" the house?) only to be summarily squashed. News of my disappearance would've made the headlines. My death would be nothing more than a strong assumption, a conclusion as unavoidable as it would have been without evidence. One moment I was present and accounted for; the next, inexplicably gone, when, in fact, I'd have become both invisible and unwelcomed.

***

The prison chaplain is a slightly pudgy, kindly man. I overheard the guards say he looked like he probably used to have his lunch money taken from him as a child. For all their chiding, he is a man of great and subtle gifts. Including my trial lawyer, he is the first person that truly understood my confession. Not that he believed how I killed. That seemed incredible even to him. What he reflected and what I began to understand for the first time was what was happening to me, how I was focused when I took their lives.

Perhaps you have had a compulsion, a desire that shreds what appeared to be the good steel net of your will, an instinct that collapses time and creates a vacuum that begs to be filled and can only be filled with a certain act, which is to say a certain reality lived through that act, the end sublimated to its means. The prison chaplain understood this, though I doubt he'd ever had such desire. It is an odd, vicious creature he knows not from experience, but from its bloody wake. When we spoke, his eyes never left mine; his expression was a combination of familiarity and loathing, as he nodded slowly and patiently absorbed my quasi-coherent ramblings, my struggle to describe being moved by fire, by a combustion of tangled emotions and rationales that nonetheless left me focused as the edge of a scalpel.

The chaplain's attentiveness never kept him from his ultimate goal of changing me. Indeed, the more he delved into me, the more he tried to "let God reclaim" my "soul." Every discussion we had, regardless of where it began, wound up in the same place. He could have been a politician. The media relations person at the company I ran would have kissed the chaplain's feet for staying so on message. Once, I asked him if prison or at least a place like prison wasn't the perfect place for someone who didn't want to engage the world and its vices. I posited to him that it was not just the controlling atmosphere, but how the lack of activities and freedom forced one to focus on the self. The chief effect of all of this was to slow time to a crawl. He asked if I'd ever heard of monasteries, said that those places had all the good and none of the bad aspects of incarceration. But then the chaplain used the subject of time to pivot onto the curious concept of eternity. From there, it was easy to speak of what he believed would happen after we die. He was sincere and oddly nonjudgmental, as if conveying the benefits of exercise or a healthy diet. When I told him I'd had all the transformation one creature could stand, he smiled and almost laughed. It was the happiest I'd ever seen him look.

As I mentioned previously, the Whistling Dragon began life as the Deep Seven. The only remnant from the old days was a music machine I never learned to operate. The first time I saw the place was on a screen. I was sitting with my biographer trying to steer the subject away from me. The program featured what I had to imagine were scenes recorded in the twentieth century. The images didn't have the full range of colors or the crisp presence of most images. The sound was different as well. You could actually tell it was coming from the screen. Moreover, the content was fascinating. If the biographer said anything during the first ten minutes or so, I certainly didn't hear her.

On screen was a man with an oversized but not life-sized doll sitting on his knee. The figure moved and spoke and, at first, I had no idea that it did so at the man's behest. It took me a moment to notice how very close they sat to one another. Then it struck me how oddly the man held his mouth while the doll spoke. When it all dawned on me, I felt stupid, almost duped. The irony of my confusion struck me like a thunderbolt. I almost doubled over with laughter. The biographer smiled, curiously.

"I thought you were old enough to have heard that joke before," she said.

In fact, I'd been so fascinated with the scene, I didn't even realize the man and dummy were telling jokes. Though, indeed, what else could they have been doing? I was able to refocus when the biographer changed the image or the channel. That is when I saw a man identified as Tyrone, the "owner" of the Deep Seven, being interviewed, reluctantly, on the street. He looked nervously between the interviewer, the camera, and the place in the background. He moved away several times, causing the reporter to finally drop all of her questions. Then there were scenes inside a place I could only assume was the Deep Seven. There were no people but, somehow, it did not seem empty. Some chairs were strewn helter-skelter and some sat around square and round tables, as if waiting for patrons. It was dim and cozy with a great deal of dark brown wood.

"There's a place with some history," my biographer said. "And speaking of history . . ." she went on, trying to revive our conversation.

It would be a while before I would see the place again. I was tempted to write, "I was a different person then." But "different" and "person" are inadequate, and incorrect respectively. The change in that time, deep as it was, was dwarfed by the change to my current form, and I am unsure if that change makes the term "person" apply to me. It is a term of convenience, whose use has been programmed rather than naturally learned.

The Deep Seven more than intrigued me. Upon seeing the bar on TV, the house in which I lived seemed suddenly less inviting. Intellectually, I had known what people meant when they used the word "sterile" to describe a living space as undesirable. But I had never felt that way about where I was living until that moment we switched the channel. Perhaps, it may have been the first inkling of the experiment fading, but the dark seemed tantalizing, warm. The space I was in seemed overlit. Even on the screen (or was it because of the screen) I could see a more human mark on that place, and was I not, at least then (and perhaps now) a human?

As much as I was attracted to it, the idea of transforming the place into something that was mine gnawed at me for months. I looked up the location and directions but there were two addresses for the same place. Then, one impulsive night, I got up from a half-eaten meal, jumped into the car, and got lost, drove past the Main Library, naturally thought of my biographer, and rambled on through neighborhoods east of Woodward Avenue. I made the mistake of stopping near the Heidelberg Project to ask directions. One group of young people with oddly colored hair at first ignored me. Some spoke amongst themselves while others gaped open-mouthed at the collection of objects—shoes, dolls, car parts, stuffed animals, et cetera—fixed onto trees and polka-dotted wooden houses and arranged in rows on vacant lots between. When I finally got their attention, they told me they were not from the area and couldn't help me.

I turned to see a young woman getting out of a car she'd just parked. She went to the rear passenger door to remove a toddler in a car seat. Surely, I thought, this woman was from the area and would know the Deep Seven. Her face tightened as I approached. She was silent for a few seconds after I asked directions. Then she looked up and asked if I was "with them," nodding to the young people. When I said no, expecting her manner to lighten, she was silent for a few more seconds before virtually spitting her words at me.

"Every time I come down to see my mother, there's somebody here for the freak show that needs directions." With that, she extricated her sleeping daughter from the car seat and carried her into the house.

After some time, I stumbled onto my destination. I don't know what I thought I would accomplish. It was locked. The street was deserted. Someone had taped a note, handwritten on cardboard, next to the padlock.

To Tyrone and Schwartz: We are so sorry to see this place closed. We thank you for all you have done and for the jukebox. We will miss you more than you know.—Your Friends, "Order of the Black Elephant"

In a flash of perhaps the purest emotion I ever felt, rivaled only by what overtook me when I was alone with my victims, I was transported back to the images of the worn dark wood I knew to be inside, the chairs I imagined as waiting. What had kept these patrons from saying goodbye in person? The cardboard note was talismanic. I had it matted and would later keep it in the safe with the deed. Even so, it passed through my hands like the place itself.

***

The Librarian

Like me, my former co-worker from the Main Branch had taken on media work as a second career. She began life as a storyteller and I could feel the sales pitch when we met to discuss the gig that would eventually get me out of prison.

"I know you're not crazy about corporations, to say nothing of working for one," she began, "but these folks have the means to bend anything to their will and a history of doing just that."

"You mean they're fascist," I replied. "Don't get me wrong. I'd almost go to work for Stalin to get out of here and I imagine their body count is lower than his."

"That's the spirit!" she encouraged.

***

The CEO

I commenced the story with what may have been a false impression. I wanted to escape my biographer not because she is a bad person but because of the nature of my biography. That also relates, in part, to why I referred to her as being unfortunate. The other part of her misfortune was her incarceration. Her previous supervisor was, I gather from her and from news reports, a bad actor: absorbed in his own ambition to the point of being comical. Nonetheless, the poor fellow did not deserve to have a solid oak door crash against his cranium, however cathartic it may have been for my biographer to have her boss truly and finally come to grips with something outside of him. In fact, despite her innermost desires, she'd had no intentions of harming him. Had he not refused her entry after summarily firing her by e-mail for no apparent reason, the door might well have stayed on its hinges. But that is more speculation on my part. I met her after what I knew was going to be a long conversation with Media Relations. Whenever they mentioned my "origins," I knew to put in an earpiece so that my hands could be free to continue work while I mostly listened.

It's been an amazing fall for everyone, including those members of Media Relations in the inner circle. Before things fell, their normal duties were suspended to safeguard my identity. Their salaries had been increased heftily. Their offices were plush, well-lit, and airy. The doors opened to but a chosen few. They don't answer their doors now either, but for very different reasons. The first day I met the VP for Media Relations, I could tell he didn't believe that I had not been human before the transformation. I told him I could offer no proof. Even the friends of the man I replaced were fooled and that had been the acid test. I did have to end one of his relationships that had become physical. He'd been involved with a woman who'd just gotten a graduate degree in business. She was a veritable fount of innovative practices, most of which I was only too happy to introduce to the firm and take credit for.

As for the man I "replaced," perhaps my first victim, how or why should I tell you about him? I could give intimate details: hair color, scent, nail rigidity, spinal curvature, organ decline, and so on. You can find the pictures online. You can find his quotes in the annual reports and see his pre-transformational interviews in company blogs. Download them, if you wish. But perhaps none of that reveals as much as the look of anguished relief on the graduate student's face when she realized the affair with him/us was over. I can also tell you that, long before I entered, he had abandoned childhood as though it were a burning building.

***

The Librarian

You will take just about any job to get out of prison. The job I was offered was not just any job. It gave me a direct connection with a CEO, a rising star in the corporate world, not my first choice. But, you may know, life isn't a series of first choices. I assumed there would be a camera crew there for the interviews I was to conduct for the bio pic of this guy. That was before I found out how reluctant the CEO was to be interviewed. I could relate. That's what helped us bond, if that's what you want to call hours of nonverbal communication. Don't get me wrong. He was never hostile or anything. In fact, he always apologized for not having a more interesting life. Those of you who haven't been under a rock for the last little while will find that apology more than ironic.

Which brings me to one of the many questions that would never have occurred to me outside of this job: is there an effective difference between discovering someone you know has been murdered and finding the body of that person? Will the nightmares be fewer or less intense? Well, of course, you say, the complete shock of an unexpected dead body has got to be greater than being told or concluding that someone has been killed. I say it depends. Maybe the nightmares cause me to say that, nightmares caused by people I came to know being found dead: executives from rival firms; people I would have never met were it not for this job; people I would have never wanted to meet were it not for this job; people whose kids and cats I played with while I waited to interview them for the biopic; people that took me to breakfast, lunch, and dinner and told me bad jokes before they got comfortable and worse jokes after they got comfortable. Maybe I want to rid myself of any smidgen of guilt for having been close, however unwittingly, to the murderer. It may be all of that combined with the sheer surprise of the whole thing, the layers of surprise. I still can't wrap my brain around what the "original" CEO and the scientists did (and this is from someone who was almost present to witness a guy birth a small elephant). They started with an assassin bug. Is that clumsy scientist-poetry or what?

***

The CEO

My programming, training, infusion, or whatever you'd label it, is, to me, at least as interesting as anything that happened afterward. Not only do I have access to the human memories but to my own, and they've been fused and supplemented. In my new form, I saw an old film that was supposed to be about the future. Much of it takes place in a year that has already passed but with none of the predicted incidents. At one point, near the end, a protagonist, on his way to the next stage in evolution, travels through what I can only describe as a traumatic array of color, a corridor of traveling hues. Part of the trauma is the relative length of time it takes the viewer to witness, or shall I say endure, this sequence. It does go on.

Now, imagine each sheet of passing color as a novel someone has read, a lecture, a formula that person has learned, a piece of information about someone he or she knows. Imagine any and all memories plying themselves into your brain with the speed of those passing colors. As you know, these are not discrete packets of knowledge. They build and interconnect and interact, and not in orderly or even logical or predictable ways. For instance, you may develop the habit of eating breakfast quickly even though you like breakfast. The person that prepares it, almost certainly your mother, takes care. Whether it's savory: eggs whipped by hand for fifteen minutes, delicately fried in butter with bits of aged cheddar, then chopped garlic and shreds of spinach thrown in just in time to barely wilt; or the meal is sweet: oatmeal cooked in milk with honey, cinnamon, and allspice, bananas and raisins, fried sliced pears on a small side plate with a glass bowl over them to keep them warm until you are ready, and the glass bowl steams up and makes a mystery of the pears—in either case, you want all the flavors at once.

But the other reason you may learn to eat quickly is that breakfast is the time your father discovers your older sister has been out all night, has come to breakfast from the outside. Young as you are, you surmise this is not like the "sleepovers" she used to attend. Your sister and father exchange what you can only discern as code, keyless as it is grim. The light in the room falls. You suddenly realize how amazingly ugly and nominal the bare bulb over the gray kitchen is, how what was supposed to be illumination conspires with the gray walls. In a moment, the room is closed off. You, your brothers and mother are listening to clutched wire coat hangers swing through the air, almost whistling. Somehow, that ghost of a sound is as clear as your sister's cries, her pleading for your father not to beat her anymore, not to kill her. The fear he has planted along with the suddenness of the beating keeps everyone in place. None of you can take your eyes from his arm slicing the air, her useless contortions to avoid the wire, the welts that rise on her hands and exposed legs and arms.

Later, as you prepare for school, you feel as though your brain has been wiped clean with fire. You happen to look toward a spot on the wall and notice a nail in the otherwise blank space where one of your school projects, a dragon made from wire, had hung. Now the tears can roll. You take the long way to school, slow and alone.

The beatings happen more than once, yet seem to happen only once. The days meld and fall over the edge. You learn to eat quickly. But, eventually, the violence spills out of the morning. There is only so much the brain can hold and precious little of that is available to the conscious mind. Most of what humans encounter goes into a reservoir, a primordial soup that slops to the surface now and again, and the incredible aromas cause what seem like unmotivated acts.

***

The Librarian

There is nothing like getting out of jail, especially if you had never been there before and didn't expect to go there in the first place. I barely remember walking up to my boss's office. I have no recollection of smashing the door off the hinges with a chair that should have been too heavy for me to lift. All of that made the trial even more surreal. That all seemed behind me when I walked with my co-worker and her uncle to their car. I was so happy; I even considered visiting my boss but realized that would be pushing it.

I had lots of questions about what had been happening while I was inside. When she visited me in prison, my former co-worker always talked about the gig on the outs that eventually persuaded the parole board to let me go. It was high enough profile and they didn't consider me a flight risk. During those visits, my co-worker promised that once I got out, she would lay out the whole story of what had happened with Ipso, the guy that birthed the little elephant with the message on its hide. I kept asking about the little girl whose school essay about the message had brought her to the attention of my boss (really, the beginning of the end, now that I look back on it). The more I asked, the more my co-worker kept telling me about the gig with the CEO and promising the other stories when I got out.

But, do I have to tell you what happened when I got out? You guessed it; the "storyteller" had no story. No fucking story, nothing about the CEO's company "acquiring" a biotech firm, or the scientists that were about to lose their jobs, or the bizarre presentation/proposal they gave to the Board to keep their jobs. That all came out later. Even so, when you're hired to do a bio for a guy that barely speaks, the clue phone should be ringing. But that's what incarceration will do for you. Don't get me wrong. It does have a tendency to put things in focus, but at the same time, ironically, it's a sharp focus with a skewed view. It's like a fetus trying to become a human. All you want is out. If I just get out, it'll be okay. The only problem is, you get out.

I didn't know I was going to work for a murderer. How was I supposed to know that? The guy had a corner office and a driver that made more than I did as a librarian. I know many of those folks are ruthless, but outright murder? I'm getting ahead. Before I get to the murders, which you can read about in detail in my book, *I Have Eaten Nothing but the Fire in My Heart* (go to the independent bookseller's site, www.indiebound.org), I want to tell you about the stuff my editor insisted I leave out. We argued about this, let me tell you. I have been trying to work this up into a screenplay of some sort.

He disappeared for a time. This was when things got pretty hot. People were missing and folks were slowly beginning to connect the dots. People in the company assumed the guy had fled to some unmapped island just west of nowhere. But I remembered how he'd once let slip that he was fascinated with this dive bar called the Deep Seven (also chronicled in my book). I was getting nowhere with his story and hadn't had much luck following up with the whole Ipso thing beyond what I already knew. So I decided to drive by the Deep Seven. I actually drove past the place a couple of times because the front of it had changed so much, that is to say expanded. The places on either side had been subsumed by what was now the Whistling Dragon. Among the myriad strange things about this place (and trust me, I know strange) was that, despite the modern, clean exterior, it was still a dive inside. Did I tell you the Deep Seven was a dive? The Deep Seven was a dive, let me tell you. I never understood how anyone walked in there without a hazmat. In the old days, when the exterior reflected the interior, you drove past quickly just to make sure nothing got on your car. It was a dive; did I mention that?

Okay, so I did go inside a few days before it was rumored to close. I did not wear a hazmat and I even had a drink. I came to check out the juke box because my coworker had some tales about that, vinyl records of classical and jazz on it, everything from Arnold Schoenberg to Julius Hemphill. But the machine wasn't even plugged in when I got there.

Anyway, getting back to the Dragon, it's strange how certain experiences shift when you try to relive them. I would have never guessed there was any significance to the CEO's reaction to a clip of Edgar Bergen and Charlie McCarthy, ventriloquist and dummy respectively. But that was one of the CEO's turning points, one of his better ones I might add.

You all know by now that he was programmed. But there was slippage. You couldn't have programmed the way he came up with the name for the place or how he thought of the place as an escape, literal or otherwise. At the same time, it seems it would take a person whose brain and guts had been merged with an insect to start karaoke night for ventriloquists, an idea so stupid it had to explode.

***

It just so happened that my first night at the Dragon I walked in on the woman with the veil holding what has come to be known as LJ or Little Jesus. I laughed till my stomach hurt and I wasn't alone, believe me. How could you not be convulsed in waves of ironic laughter when Jesus is a puppet singing like a dolphin with a cross duct taped to his back; when the woman making him sing is all in white, including a veil, but for red gloves, a red waistband, and red high-tops; when there are Band-Aids in the palms of his hands where the spikes went in? And what was "he" singing? It was an old hillbilly spiritual:

> Glory, glory hallelujah
> When I lay my burden down
> All my troubles will be over
> When I lay my burden down

Some of the trendily dressed young folks there stared in rapt wonder, creeped out and fascinated. Acts waiting to go on, or who had been on before her, sat poker-faced, though I sensed a grim enviousness. Some had writing pads, others had computers, and they seemed to literally note her every move. It was all too funny and, naturally, alcohol didn't remove the comic element for me. Halfway through a Long Island Iced Tea, I realized I was going to have to walk out right then or have someone call EMS. My stomach still hurt the next morning.

The next morning was also when the true sadness of that song she sang hit me. How many times had I heard my grandmother sing it and let the words wash over me, meaningless as stained glass, never realizing the singer's only joy comes with death, or so she hopes. It wasn't until then that I remembered I had come to the bar to find the CEO. I had to admit the Veiled Woman had power.

***

The CEO

I booked other ventriloquists at the Dragon besides the Veiled Woman, just as one could say there are other classical composers besides Beethoven. It was her video on the web that brought the place notoriety of every shade. Certain religious types were on her side, though her songs were often cryptic. Many came to see her because her work was cryptic. Cryptic or not, I noticed a shift in the crowd. It was the day she arrived with two cases. LJ was in one. She pulled him out and began singing a spiritual about sin, but stopped half way through. She laid LJ down and called for help from the audience. A young man with a shaved head walked to the stage area, opened the other case, and pulled out a female puppet that was naked except for paper leaves over its breasts and crotch. He helped her get both puppets ready, propping them on her knees. There was much expectation. What would the new puppet sing? Would the voice that spoke through it be even higher than LJ's?

LJ and the Veiled Woman looked at Eve silently for a few too many seconds. Then the VW nodded and very somber music engulfed the room like fog. Eve rose slowly from her chair into a hotter part of the stage light as LJ began the aria, even though the VW sang with her own female voice. I would later learn it was "Casta Diva" from *Norma*, an opera by Bellini. The aria was a plea, a supplication to a goddess.

As she sang in Italian, it took a few days for the controversy to surface. But when it was out that "Little Jesus" was pleading with "Eve," certain religious types stopped coming. Others took the VW to task. They interrogated and shouted. With every encounter, she would wait until there was quiet and end with the same question. "What would Jesus do, who would he be if there was no sin?"

***

What happened to me in Texas, specifically, Galveston, was an off and on mystery, but it was the first clue that my own transformation was flawed, temporary. Those born with my original form, my original species, are far more prevalent in Texas, in the southwest United States in general. There are a few of us (them?) in Michigan but not in the urban areas. As for the company, geography was immaterial. We sold value we suspected would exist to people we never met. Such an operation is unfettered by location.

One of the other important items to note about my firm is the acquisition. My scientists were originally employed by a biotech firm, whose purchase was financed through leverage. The company was about to be sold again to another biotech firm. That transaction would have made my scientists redundant. They had, however, great confidence and held great store in the process that eventually facilitated my transformation.

It had not initially occurred to them that the process may have no good practical use. Only in the midst of creating their presentation to the Board did they begin to ask themselves how or why anyone could or would make use of the merging of humans with insects, to say nothing of who would be the transferee. It almost took them longer to answer those questions than it did to create the process in the first place. But, after watching a cartoon about a singing frog that refuses to sing when his ostensible owner would be paid for the performance, they stumbled upon the idea of reverse engineering the process to create an insect with human consciousness and using the creature as an industrial spy. Of course, the Board thought US intelligence agencies would pay just as much, if not more, than the private sector and would be at much lower risk of scandal.

With that, they needed but one more component. Then they found him, us, me.

***

The Librarian

Before the CEO was a CEO, he was a factory worker. Records, mostly police records, show he arrived from Texas and wandered around Detroit like a blind dog in a meat house, as my grandmother used to say, didn't know if he wanted to shit or go fishing. All-night poker, tours of topless bars and dope houses, blind pigs, you name it. How he managed only short stints in the joint is beyond me.

One day, somehow, he winds up on the east side of Detroit. One thing you have to know about Detroit, there is ghetto and there is slum. Don't get me wrong. I'm not one of these white folks who's unaware of racism, the Detroit metro area being the most segregated in the US. But one of the first questions two Detroiters meeting for the first time will ask one another is "you from the east side or the west side?" There are good pockets on the east side. But most of the lower east side that wasn't destroyed by I-75 or "urban renewal" is slum. That is where our hero found himself one Sunday morning, in an abandoned car near the door of a storefront church on Cadillac Street (if a filtered, somewhat secondhand memory is to be believed). Did

I mention that he was a white guy in a black neighborhood a few weeks after the city's riot that left forty-two dead?

He was discovered by a middle-aged black woman who had left church early to go to a union meeting. He was sleeping with his back against the door of the car. She stepped outside just as the hinges gave way and he fell out onto the sidewalk, bloody and gagging on his own spit. She went back inside and called an ambulance. Have you ever waited for an ambulance in a large, urban, mostly African-American area after a riot? She eventually got some folks to take him inside. She went to her meeting and didn't think she would see him again.

The storefront church pastor tried to sober him up and decided to send his family home while he watched over the drunk that had landed at the church doorstep. It would be the pastor's contribution to healing the racial rift that had managed to grab folks' attention.

The woman that found him, the union rep, was not happy about her pastor staying behind. She had convinced the preacher to come with her to the meeting directly after church. She'd been hounding him day in, day out, trying to get him to meet with black union members, a militant offshoot who'd gathered to fight racism in the union. Some folks were reluctant to join. But she knew if she got even one preacher to back them, doors would open.

His church was small, but the pastor's influence on the east side in particular was phenomenal. There were folks in the surrounding block clubs who claimed to be church members but rarely showed up. Maybe it was guilt, but these folks voted based on his recommendations and went to the PTA meetings at his urging, did everything but go to church. There were others who felt beholden to him who had no pretense of going to that church or any other. But their relatives had been snatched from heroin addiction by his street ministry. The guy had pull.

She'd shown up at the church that morning totally excited about the preacher meeting with her and her friends after the service. But now, the preacher was watching over this guy from nowhere. The idea of closing the loop on all the things she cared about seemed lost. And it was the fault, of all things, of a drunken white man falling out of an abandoned car. Why the hell did he have to come all the way over to the east side to show his ass? Didn't they have bars in Melvindale?

***

The CEO

I mentioned the graduate student earlier, how I (and the CEO as well) stole ideas from her. But she was not the first woman that moved him; there was a black woman, a socialist (though she never admitted to such). He was not long arrived in Detroit and was about to exhaust his meager savings when he stumbled upon her. Actually, she stumbled upon him as he all but fell into her lap.

He was found in a quite foul state near the church she attended. The pastor of the church took him in and eventually tried help the CEO-to-be to find his home. He even enlisted the aid of the Women's Auxiliary to supply the man with decent meals. This somehow enraged the woman who'd found the CEO. Her rage blossomed into an altercation that caused her to leave the church. Certainly, she thought she'd seen the last of that particular drunken white man. But, with the help of the pastor, the man was hired by the factory where the woman worked.

One day, in the cafeteria, she was surreptitiously handing out leftist literature. The man was sitting next to another white worker who asked the woman what she was handing out. The inquiring man didn't wait for an answer but grabbed a flyer. The woman was infuriated but wanted to maintain a low profile. She scowled but said nothing. Our hero suddenly recognized her and was about to speak as she turned to walk away. Then the man who'd snatched her flyer spoke up.

"This seems like some communist stuff to me," he said with a lilting, melodious southern accent while smirking at the flyer. "They wouldn't 'low this where I come from."

"Then why don't you go back to where you come from?" the woman spat out. "I'll tell you why," she retorted before he could answer, "because you wouldn't have a pot to piss in or a window to throw it out of. That mammy-made Mississippi crap is backwards as the day is long and they got the poverty to prove it. You wanna bring sharecropping and outhouses up here and we ain't going for it."

In mere moments, she had removed whatever vestiges of homesickness the man who was to become CEO had. But her seriousness also made his northern days of drinking, gambling, and sex seem all the more wasteful. It was no longer a sin against a God he'd never known, but somehow it still seemed a betrayal. Over and above what she said, the passion of her delivery, the shape of the words that left her mouth, merged with her glorious soft eyes. She was beautiful in a way he could not imagine another woman being beautiful at that moment. Even the color of her skin, which he knew to be an obstacle to his wish fulfillment, was at once unique and immaterial. She was who she was. There could be no one like her and he had to find a way to be with her.

***

I gave the union woman's diary to my biographer. I don't know if she read it or remembers reading it. I did not see her for a few days afterward. It was a particularly bad moment for the biographer. The father of a child she knew had killed himself. It was unclear how the child discovered her father was dead. It was, as you may have surmised, the Girl who said she deciphered the so-called message on the hide of the small, long elephant birthed by that other truly unfortunate creature. It seemed nothing but tragedy came in his wake.

I vaguely recall some shooting incident perpetrated by a factory worker fired because he was unable to focus on his job. He'd become wholly obsessed with deciphering the "message" on the elephant. In any event, after the Girl's father died, my biographer returned to her task a changed woman. She was at once more relaxed and, to my great but short-lived relief, less focused on me. If only her state of mind had lasted.

***

The Librarian

Coming out of prison, I thought I had a good grip on my perspective. The fact is I pretty quickly fell back into normal mode except for doing whatever it took not to go back in. Then, I found myself holding the Girl, a thirteen-year-old orphan, at her father's funeral. It was a short affair. The longest part was the drive to the cemetery. A bunch of us got lost. We couldn't have a car procession, some new ordinance based on cuts to the police budget. I passed the Heidelberg Project, slowed down, wanted to stop, wanted to get lost in the colors and rows and rows of discarded things people once thought were going to make them happy. I got to the gravesite just as they were lowering the casket. The Girl sat in a row of folding chairs in front of the grave, her head buried in someone's lap.

Later, the woman I recognized as her teacher came up to me with a conspiratorial look. She had arranged for the Girl to visit her and even spend some overnights. The Girl had also requested to visit me. (She had tried to visit me in prison, but couldn't get a ride.) Sadly, the Girl's family was only too glad to make the arrangement. I couldn't figure out why they seemed to want nothing to do with her. But it left me hollow inside.

As you know, I got to spend quite a bit of time with her during the Black Elephant debacle. She told me the whole fairy-tale story of her mother passing away and how much she missed her. The ugly story got an ugly coda when I met her father and discovered he was a true and unique asshole. But she was always anxious to see him at the end of the day and grieved his loss as deeply and profoundly as I have seen anyone grieve.

Having her over was a serious adjustment. As you might guess, I'm not in a palace. What's more, I never had kids, and now here I am with one going through trauma and puberty (who can tell the difference?) at the same time. It was a good thing school was almost out. At first, all she did was cry and sleep. Now she just writes reams and reams in notebooks. On second thought, school may be better.

Days passed before the Girl talked to me unsolicited. Mostly, she left notes. So I began to leave her notes too, at first about simple stuff. Finally, I took the plunge and asked what she was writing about. That killed the "conversation" for a few more days.

Then, out of the blue, one Saturday afternoon during a late lunch, I turned on the radio. It happened to be the CBC and the opera was on. "*Traviata!*" she shouted, pushed back her chair, and began twirling around the room. She grabbed me out of my chair. I tried to waltz with her, barely remembered the moves, and ended up with a sort of polka hybrid. But it worked. We danced around the room until what she later told me was "the drinking song" ended.

"It was my mother's favorite," she told me as she plopped back into her chair. Then she was up again, into the bedroom for a few moments, and emerged with two notebooks. They were full of writing, front and back pages, with notes in the margins, and dog-eared, food stained, and, I suspect, tear-stained as well. Every word and paragraph was her mother, what she wore, what she liked to eat, driving habits, education, how she talked when she was excited, the way she held her mouth when something puzzled her, it was all there. I was going to make a joke about seeking out dental records when she asked if doctors gave out information about their patients. Sections of her notebooks reminded me of the interminable list section in *Moby Dick* but, her intro was good.

My Mother in Words

I wanted to resurrect my mother with words and with what can't be spoken. You and I will work together. I will make her present. You will draw her picture with the music in your head. I will take you into the rooms where we all danced.

***

The CEO

The CEO's father stumbled back into what he thought was his son's life like a dazed beast onto a firing range. I, we, recognized him in the hotel vaguely before the air around him pulsed red. I saw him while riding down in a glass elevator from the hotel suite where the event was held, then again from an interior

balcony of the hotel. Strange they would dress janitors in white
shirts and pants, but there he was with his red-and-blue cap, a
broom, a long-handled dust pan, and the hotel's circular logo
on his back.

I was about to discover the instrument and a memory.
The former was a cylindrical organ that felt as though it was
attached to the base of my spine. That was anatomically impossible, of course. The instrument slept in my throat, efficiently
stored and dormant until the proper moment. The memory also
slept, but in a far deeper recess.

***

Years ago, as a child, the CEO we were to become was returning home from school. It was towards the end of winter, a
surprisingly warm day even for Texas. He removed his jacket
and almost skipped home past his friends. While he didn't
smile, his buoyancy was evident. He arrived at his small wood
shingle house to discover the shades drawn and the windows
closed. This, he thought, required correction. The sun and sky
were too inviting and brilliant to be stopped by such gloomy,
trivial barriers. As soon as he let himself in, he called out, got
no reply, dumped his coat on the living room couch, and began
going through the house, making sure there was light and air
in all the rooms downstairs. He didn't dare ascend to his father
and mother's attic bedroom. Satisfied that the small grayish
house had released most of its shadows and stale air, he began
rummaging the bread box and refrigerator, taking care not to
disturb food designated exclusively for his father. Though he
thought no one would miss a spoonful of the half gallon of ice
cream that had already been scooped.

He heard feet half stumbling down the stairs and fumbled to
replace the lid on the ice cream, get it all back into the freezer,

and clean and replace the eating utensils before the door to the attic swung open. He was still rinsing the spoon when his father appeared, bleary-eyed, in the kitchen doorframe.

"What you been eating?"

"I just found this spoon in the sink and rinsed it."

"Don't let me catch you in something you ain't supposed to be." The father turned his head toward the living room and his eyes suddenly popped open. "What did I tell you about the couch?"

Stones fell into the boy's stomach as he struggled to recall which rule he may have violated.

"Where are you supposed to put your coat when you come in?"

The boy dropped the spoon he realized he was still holding when he saw his father begin to loosen his belt. Just as suddenly, the man stopped and dove with surprising agility to grab something on the floor under one of the kitchen chairs. As he bent down, he passed close enough for the boy to catch the smell of beer. The father got to his feet clutching the tangle of wire coat hangers that were the remnants of the boy's school project.

My scientists were supposed to have transferred every memory. Every detail was to have been at my immediate disposal. It was the only way I could convincingly take on the life of the CEO. I had dates, times, where he and others stood at various moments, details he could never have pulled to the surface. As I relived the memory of the beating the CEO took as a boy, I realized there are memories and there are memories. Seeing his father popped the lid on a charred crusty pot that had been quietly boiling for decades.

***

The Librarian

As you know, the juiciest parts of the CEO's life never made it to the script for the biopic I was assigned to write. For example, it wasn't until the trial that we found out that the CEO's father had not been randomly assigned to clean the hotel where his son was being honored. The father asked for the assignment to clean that building. He hadn't been in contact with his son for years but saw him in the newspaper, one of those local-kid-is-rich-so-now-we-love-him stories. The father started bragging to his coworkers about his son, the big shot. Naturally, they felt even sorrier for him. Only occasionally was he truly sober, and even then, he had winding, untenable stories to tell.

He managed to trade building assignments with a guy that owed him a favor. He wanted to be there when his son spoke and made all those bigwigs bow down. What he somehow hadn't counted on was being too busy to get to the ballroom where the event was. But, no matter, he and his "son" were indeed reunited.

***

The CEO

He did not see my face until it was too late. I had watched him wheel a pail of soapy water into the men's room. He'd put a barrier at the door to indicate it was closed for cleaning. I went in and latched the door behind me. His smile lasted perhaps a second before he stumbled backward over the toilet, voiceless in his horror as I tried to speak. But the instrument held my tongue and I realized he could see it protruding from my mouth.

I had wanted to tell him the exact time of day that he'd beaten me, what we were both wearing, the rooms where I'd left blood on the walls, how I'd almost knocked myself out as I ran from him looking backwards and rammed my head into the edge of an open door. I wanted to ask him why he'd dropped the coat hangers he had been using to beat me. But, in the oddest moment, I suddenly thought the wires would leave cuts that would be visible in the short sleeves I would soon be wearing, whereas his fists had struck me mostly beneath my clothes, or maybe the wire had begun to cut his hand. Did he remember how many days it would take me to get out of bed afterward, to say nothing of being able to walk to school?

Those thoughts and inquiries spun and raced inside me but I could utter nothing. Our mouths were joined. I heard small, rhythmic, involuntary sounds that may have come from him, from me, or the two of us grinding together. The instrument had parted his lips, broken his front teeth, and probed his insides, searching for internal organs to disconnect them like reluctant, unripe fruit being snapped from a tree.

***

The Librarian

Another thing revealed at the CEO's trial was that the original, (all) human CEO only consented to the transformation because he thought certain memories would be wiped from his head.

***

The CEO

I took his key and discreetly locked the restroom door behind me. It was the next day before anyone tried to open the room and later still before his body was discovered. It was in a stall far from the door, face down in the toilet. The person who'd come to clean thought he may have drowned, somehow, until he saw the skin shrunken around the skull.

The son had rarely spoken of his father or any family. All printed biographic material began with his rise in Detroit. The father's years of desperate drinking had obscured much of his physical resemblance to his son, so no one made that connection. Their worlds had come apart.

The death became news only after I was back in Detroit and even then was only local. That gave me much relief at that time. Identifying the body or acting bereaved would have required more resources than I have. The mere sight of even his corpse may well have caused the instrument to swell. This was the only murder to which I wanted to confess and found myself somehow unable to do so. It was as if there was another instrument, an instrument of the psyche that refused to own the act as a crime, refused to let me to speak the truth of it, even as the words darted within me and clawed for release.

***

The Girl

While the Librarian was busy with the trial, I wandered the apartment and found some diaries, dozens of notebooks. At first, I thought they were hers and then I realized how old they were, referencing the '67 riot and the Renaissance Center being built. Actually, there were lots of things in them that didn't exist anymore. It was not that long ago, but it felt so old. I almost wanted to go through them and add notes in the margins about what had changed or had not happened as she thought it would.

It was clear whoever had written them worked in the factory and was deep in the union. It seemed like she had two jobs. She was busy and the entries were sporadic.

She found a man passed out drunk who fell out of an abandoned car. She wrote some pretty mean things about him even though she was on drugs at one time herself. She did help save him from being drunk all the time. She'd had no one to find her and take her into a safe place like she did for him. She dropped drugs Miles Davis–style, cold turkey, locked away in a room in the house of a true friend; used what was left of her will to close off any escape routes or tunnels; and, unlike Miles, she never went back. The room was bigger than the walls.

There is a diary entry about Belle Isle, a picnic, a family reunion. I could not tell from the words how old she was, but not very. But she was swinging on a playground close to twilight. Did she know how dark it was getting? Who knows? But, on her way back to everyone else, she lost her way or ran into a man she thought she knew or both. He said her family was looking for her. She thought he was taking her back to them. But once there was no one else around, he slowed down, began walking too close, and was on her with a suddenness that snatched her breath away. He asked her strange questions like why had she walked with him in the dark? The question and the pain of the rocks at her back finally made her cry out, though he'd threatened to kill her if she did. A group of men, not long off work, still in their security guard uniforms, playing cards by headlights on the other side of some bushes came around and through the bushes. He didn't run. They had to pull him off of her and fought over whether or not to beat him bloody.

***

The diaries reminded me of my father. I don't think he ever spoke a complete sentence. The words, commas, and periods were usually in the right places. But there was always a silent part that needed to be filled in. It was not the gaps between the times that he spoke or the days between diary entries. It was the words he spoke and the entries themselves that hold the spaces. Before they were married, my mother's job was to help him. She was not there so much to fill in the spaces but to help him realize they were there, where he'd left something out and had continued on as if everything was in place. My father never really got over the death of his brother or the deaths of his friends in the factory during a shooting incident. It was my mother that showed him how empty space connected those things and the space behind the sadness that never seemed to leave after my uncle died. The gaps in the union lady's diary have that sadness. She is raped. Then she spends a lot of time in church. Then she gets a job in the factory and discovers beer and other drugs that become her new church. Finally, she locks herself away for days. Food and water are placed in the room when she's asleep. Only the tiny bathroom window remains unsealed.

***

The Union Representative

While I was away, locked in the room, shaking like an old car on a bad road and throwing up everything I ever ate, they fired me. At first, I begged for my job. I agreed to meet one of the foremen at a bar to talk it over. Big mistake, not only did I almost accept his offer for a drink, but, even after I refused, he tried to snuggle up close to me in the booth. I stared dead into his face, pulled out the stiletto my daddy gave me and snapped the blade out. Then I used the knife to cut the meat on my plate. The foreman slid away and called for the check.

***

I went to the union hall today, like Justine told me to do a while ago. I met with this old Polish guy whose last name I couldn't pronounce if they put a gun to my head. He kept calling me honey, but he calls everybody honey or sister. Anyway, he had me fill out a bunch of papers while he was on the phone. Every call started with, "I got this colored girl over here they fired and I need to get her back."

***

I almost end up near 12th and Clairmount the other night, about two blocks from where everything jumped off. The news is driving me crazy. Not even the one black reporter (working serious overtime) knows anything about the places he's talking about. Passing judgment and dodging bullets and that's the ones who got the short straw and ended up on the street. Let's not even talk about the ones at their desks. But I can't stop watching or listening to it because I have to know what's happening besides folks calling to tell me what's going on. I thought this mess would be over after a couple of days. Damn fools burning their own damn places. Where the hell we gonna shop? My father called and said he was going to come get me but called back about fifteen minutes later and said he kept getting stopped by the police and turned back to the house. Just as well. I'm as safe here as I am there. Though I would love to sit down and let them fix me something. Some honey-baked chicken with some macaroni and cheese and cornbread from the pan and I wouldn't care about nothing for a minute.

***

Stan, the old Polish guy, got put in a bit of a trick bag today. His white friends were teasing him about me in front of his wife, man old enough to be my damn granddaddy. But he speaks up for folks on the floor and in the union hall and they can't stand it, especially since the riot. He's pushing for Bernard and Calvin who should have been in skilled trades long-ass time ago and everybody knows it, just don't want to let black men move up, even when they do right. People have started saying shit right out in the open, acting like every black person is a sniper and these supposed to be our union brothers.

***

Another bad day, near miss at the plant handing out literature. I had to lay into one of those crackers trying to talk shit like it was the good old days in the south. I thought I was going to have to slap him but his friend, or somebody I thought was his friend, jumped between us. Young and looked like Paul Newman but skinny as hell. He kept staring at me and trying to smile but seemed like he was afraid. Then I recognized him.

***

Stan finally gave it up today. His oldest called me to the hospital. The sun was out for the first time in days and when I opened the door to the hospital room it blinded me for a second. Everybody was there, even the new foreman. I was so glad all the tubes and wires and machines were gone, even if he didn't look like himself. His grandson and wife couldn't stop crying and that was really sad.

I drifted back to the time me and him played cards in a vacant lot over on the east side. He went with me to talk with some of the hospital security guards I knew from the attack on Belle Isle, trying to get them to start a real union. Stan must have been the only white man in miles that wasn't a store owner.

I touched his hand before I walked out of the room. I would have give my arm to hear him call me honey.

***

I almost don't believe it, but they voted me into Stan's slot today. And guess who it was working with Justine to get the Mexicans and the Arabs to vote with the black folks? I may have misjudged the guy, even after the lunchroom incident. I still can't feature me and a white guy going out together, especially *this* white guy. I don't like folks staring. He was surprised to find out I'm in recovery. I can tell he's new to the meetings because a veteran would know I show all the classic signs, flaring and working too much. It's hard to let go.

***

I had to get on Justine today about all her teasing about being with a white guy. I told her she just wanted to make an Oreo. It was a joke and she laughed but it was a hard, sharp laugh and then she said I was sick. I laughed that off but it hurt me. It hurt me deep. I drove over there after work and we talked about stuff that hadn't come up for years. I finally told her everything was really good but that he still seems young. Justine just smiled and asked, since when is that a problem?

***

Everything's changed now, more real. It happened. That's all I know. It was one day but it was more than a day. Everything really turned when we kissed. Nothing meant anything any-more. I know that sounds bad. The problem is I want to write about this thing but I can't, not really.

It started with us both deciding to skip church even though neither of us said it out loud. Looking back, I know it was just me. Lately, going to church meant driving fifteen minutes try-ing to find somewhere to park. The people were nice, but there were too many of them to know who they really were.

Anyway, it was the kiss. He always had nice lips, especially for a white boy. But that morning, after we had suddenly stopped getting dressed, I felt his hand stroke my cheek. His skin was rough but his hand was gentle and cool to the touch. When I looked into his eyes, I couldn't help but close mine. They were closed when we moved together, when our lips touched. It felt like we were having sex right at that moment. When we did, everything rushed together. Something came to me. It felt like what happens sometimes with the music at church, I'm danc-ing outside of my body and my voice is gone. This time, it was the silence even though I could hear everything. It was bright even with my eyes closed. The sheets on the bed felt different. I could smell the sun in them like when mama used to take them off the line in the summer. I stopped thinking. All the words disappeared from my head. I was only making love at that moment in that room and even that was fine because the room didn't really hold me anymore. Nothing was outside of me. I didn't have to look at the sun or sky or river or know what the birds sang. I was there.

*****

It's almost like when I was using, only instead of being blurred, everything is clear. Even so, I almost ran into a moving hi-lo the other day. I used to feel like I was dying waiting for the weekend. But the names of weekdays are just names now. The sun comes and goes like it always has. I know when I'm supposed to be at the plant, but time is one long river.

***

Is it my fault? I have given up trying to explain to him why I don't have to go to church, why no one has to go. It's all inside (and outside for that matter). I thought he'd be happy since he doesn't really know God, he just fears God. Like work, he only goes because he's afraid not to. These days, he's either at work or church. He's taking every bit of overtime he can get and doesn't have any time for us. He tracks every penny. Making money takes time and you've only got so much time. I remember when my father started working like that. It wasn't long before he had a heart attack, and even if he hadn't, he and my mother had started fussing. You need time, not just to talk, but to sit and say nothing.

***

I finally convinced Justine that we had to make that move, go to the newspapers with the story to force them to hire more black men into skilled trades. Even if we only get in the Chronicle, we can't wait on the union another second. It's so in our face. My folks think I am not as concerned because I don't yell anymore but I got everything uptight. I can see where the cracks are. I know what lies management's going to tell before they tell them. I feel like I am around the corner before they know it's time to turn.

***

He may be coming around to his old self. I would be in heaven then. He brought me proof that management lied about not getting Jimmy's doctor's notice before they disciplined him.

Justine asked how he got that info. I don't want to think about it.

***

I finally learned how to do the honey-baked chicken he likes. So I cooked a whole bird even though he's MIA and it just made me think about him all the more. It's the closest I've been to being truly sad since that day everything opened up after we made love. I'm afraid of what's going to happen to him once work and church can't pass the days for him anymore. It's good and bad that he's not on the shop floor. Even before everything became clear, I knew people weren't made to be in the factory. But at least there you make something besides money.

The last time we were really together, he tried to pretend the problem was me not going to church, not being my old self. All of a sudden, a question jumped to the front of my brain and, before I knew it, I almost shouted: "What the hell is an 'old self'?"

The Antecedent Blues

1. One Such Bird or What's Really in There?

Once, there was a bird whose call was the sound of the human chest cavity being cracked open, a sound usually heard by heart surgeons and those who worked with them. That sound was followed by, or seemed connected to, sometimes, very rarely, the sound of sloshing that was the movement of liquids in the body on the operating table when the breastbone had been particularly thick or stubborn, and the body had to be wrestled with a bit, thus causing its various liquids to slosh about both inside and outside the body depending, of course, on the width of the chest opening. That sound was followed by a slightly more melodious sound. Though, indeed, virtually anything would seem slightly more melodious in comparison.

In any event, that other sound, the second or third sound, depending on if it was followed by the sloshing, was a cackling, whistling sound, or at least that is how lay people described it, because ornithologists had a very long and scientific description that no one else used. The cackling, whistling second or third sound also could have been someone speaking very quickly, repeating the question, "What's really in there? What's really in there?"

Of course, this sounded nothing like a parrot or other talking birds. Some denied that it sounded like words at all, and for them it was an earworm relentlessly dogging them during dreaming or waking. The worst of the bunch had the sloshing before the voices. Yes, there were multiples, asking, "What's really in there?" repeatedly, sometimes with annoying irregular gaps between and sometimes with hints of the sloshing.

The wealthier ones with the earworm issue, a decidedly disproportionate but by no means exclusive sector of that population, hired people to kill as many of these birds as possible. Older and more confused members of the earworm group, those who did not wander in front of transports and kill themselves or wind up in virtual comas, had some vague fear and memory of something called "the endangered species list" and secretly worried that the birds might be put on it if too many were killed. That was a baseless concern and one that, in any event, did not plague most of their ilk.

Anyway, these birds had once been in the tropical climes exclusively but began coming further and further north as the Earth heated and corpses began to mount in the brown hemisphere from heat and storms. That is not our concern.

This is the story of a girl who, at first, only knew about these things through video implants and screens and one such bird she happened to take in as a pet. It would be more correct to say that the bird lived with her for a while. She called it a pet because she'd never had a pet, had only seen pets in videos and didn't realize that even the people from the last century had stopped using that word to refer to non-humans that lived with them. But that may have been difficult for even a smart child to discern.

She was indeed a smart child. Her mother wrote books, though very few people read them, and her father did something scientific with the innards of video implants or their plasma or both that related to how we see and perceive digital video, how we are now absorbed in it the way we used to be absorbed with each other and with trees and clouds and things like that.

His explanations of his work were hypnotic in that, a few seconds after he began talking, a narcotic drowsiness overcame even the most alert listener. Only his coworkers had the vaguest outline of what the company paid him to do.

But everyone understands what an author is or does or has some idea that such a person uses words to communicate ideas even if those ideas are at times obscured by their expression. Such was the case with the Girl's mother, whose work was praised unceasingly by people who had even more difficulty earning money than she did.

At one point, her husband's company was sold to another company and, try as he might, her husband found himself unable to explain, and thereby justify, what it was he did. The people in the newly formed personnel department and even their supervisors ended up with their heads on the table or slumped in their chairs minutes after he began talking. They had scheduled meetings with him because they'd even become sleepy when they'd tried to engage his video presentations. They didn't realize that his actual speech brought on a level of stupor rivaled only by the most powerful drugs. One unfortunate executive had to recuse herself from assessing his work altogether, because whether she engaged his presentations or his voice, she had flashbacks of lapsing into a coma from a rare tropical illness.

There were two other scientists at the newly formed company who had some interest in trying to harness and sell this infectious, narcoleptic ability. But they were too busy working on their own discovery. They had found a way to merge humans with insects, a project they thought might save their jobs despite the merger. So the husband of the Author was left to his own brain-deadening devices.

The effect on the family income was such that the Author had to step up and try to write a traditional story, one that would attract more than academics that were just shy of inducing the sort of boredom so deftly brought on by her husband. It was not easy for her.

Morning after morning, she would rise early and try to create a straight narrative and to resist lapsing into obscure poetics.

> i read the tornado
> to see why we're invisible
> when the puzzle shakes out
> and the stars all shout
> but i'm still in doubt

She did feel herself getting closer to being able to construct stories that might attract the money of large numbers of people when she began reading fairy tales at night to prepare for the next morning's writing. It brought her poetry more down to earth.

> horse racing seemed simple at a glance
> but oh the rolling quake of hooves
> the dirt flying and sanctifying
> the electric silk of the jockey uniforms
> making them like some

overgrown sprites astride
four-legged juggernauts
and all of it balanced
on the point of a wager
a guess
on who could go a certain distance
before the rest
each rider assigned a beast

It was during this phase in her writing that the Author began to notice strange sounds. But it was summer, and as bad as the air outside had become, they could no longer afford climate control, and it was the duty of the first person who woke to open the windows. With the windows open, it was hard to tell where the sound was coming from. But after a few days of distraction, she decided she had to find the source of the sound and stop it if she could. The investigation led her to her daughter's room.

Standing outside the door, the Author assumed the Girl must have been screening something odd. Actually, the family wasn't much for video, so most screen fare seemed as odd to them as their Author and Scientist work was to most other people. But this sound seemed both odd and familiar. The Author recalled an audio news item just as she knocked on her daughter's door.

When the Girl opened the door, the bird, perched in the open window, loudly seemed to ask, "What's really in there? What's really in there?" Fortunately, its head was poking in the room and its butt was outside, because the bird delivered each question with massive droppings.

The Author was happy that the bird's waste fell outdoors. But she wanted the entire bird to be outdoors. It startled her, and the sound it made was even more startling, off-centered. It did not look like a bird that should be able to talk, like a parrot or myna, and that, combined with the that fact it didn't even look real—it was pudgy with a short beak, pink feathers, and blue-tipped wings—made it feel like it could have been a chicken or, for that matter, a chipmunk talking. Its voice seemed like a Frankenstein part grafted on to it, something that worked against the laws of nature.

You have probably guessed that the Girl felt quite differently about the bird. While she was also glad its butt was sticking out of the window when it dropped its load, that was about the only point of agreement she and her mother had on the creature.

The Girl was a great reader who had trouble hearing. She had awoken one morning thinking her hearing was normal because the bone-cracking call of the bird pulled her from sleep like nothing ever had. The source of the sound was just as startling as the sound itself, for she recognized the bird from a painting she'd seen in a picture book about communists (*Don't Try This at Home*), a picture of a woman and a man holding hands, the man's strange eyes and disproportionate size relative to the small woman whose head was tilted at a slight angle that somehow matched her quizzical smile and her eyebrows being almost one line. Above her, with a banner in its beak, was a pink bird with blue-tipped wings that seemed too chubby to fly, a feathery carnival prize come to life just for the painting.

It had taken days for the Girl to make out the sounds that followed the breaking noises, which she did not associate with the sound of bones cracking. The sounds following the breaking noise were quieter and quicker. They were almost whispers, reminding her of how her parents sounded when they were arguing, which was often, and not wanting her to know they were arguing.

She could tell that her mother thought the bird was as startlingly ugly as she thought it beautiful. What to do?

"The first time I heard it, I thought my hearing was fixed," said the Girl in as matter-of-fact a manner as she could.

The mother wasn't sure about the hearing part. She was sure that the Girl so loved the bird that she associated it with healing. The Author fought her inclination to kill the bird with the heaviest, sharpest object she could find, bury it, or better still, pay someone to incinerate it with an added bonus if they provided proof of its demise. Instead, she bent her unsteady knees and clasped the Girl in her arms.

***

After the Girl had run away to be with a group of musicians—real, barely legal, live performing musicians—the Author would often replay the scene with the bird in her head. It had been the most connected moment she and the Girl had had since the Author had birthed her, and the only one both of them could share. For the rest of her life, the Author alternately regretted and second-guessed her choice to write about musicians.

But here it should be noted that the Girl didn't exactly run away, or it didn't exactly feel like running away. The Girl's hearing was thought to be bad, but it was simply extraordinary in a somewhat dysfunctional way. To her ears and mind, the Bird's chest-cracking sound was slightly muffled percussion, and the questions that followed (if there was not sloshing) were singing—a pleading, plaintive singing—but singing nonetheless, and singing that called to her in a way nothing else had.

After days and nights of pondering the sound, sometimes losing sleep over it (why did it matter to her so?), she somehow

imagined or decided the Bird was not the original source of
the sound, but that it was imitating someone, a human that
it had once been with. She imagined it at the window of a
singer, day after day silently absorbing the rigorous practice,
or thrilling the singer with its imitations of her. The singer she
imagined was a woman younger than her mother, who looked
a bit like her mother and perhaps even a bit like the Girl, and
who sounded like her mother but with a deeper, clearer voice
that when pushed had a bit of an edge to it.

This Singer in the Girl's mind did not hold back much in
singing or in life in general and the Bird, being a bird, had
no way of knowing or interpreting the emotion that swirled
around the room. So, before it sang, it emitted a percussive
sound to get the attention of the listener, to say *oye*, hear ye
hear; bright, loud beats in the place of welcoming trumpets.

Then the Bird would really open up, and the voice of the
Singer was somehow more plaintive coming from something
that looked like it rose from the drawing of a child that couldn't
resist combining unlikely colors or making the wings so chubby
that they brought to mind feathered bees, rotund, with blue
and pink stripes.

In the run up to the running away, the Girl had begun to read
some of her mother's work. It made her ponder.

> it is not magic that keeps the vampire
> from seeing itself in the mirror
> it is blinded
> by the only appetite it has ever known

"You know mom, I don't get the vampire thing," the Girl
began one of her interrogations. "I mean, this poem feels serious but, vampires?"

"It's just a stand in for people who run the society and please don't go repeating that outside of the home," her mother admonished.

"And we're supposed to know that how? Seriously, I could recite this poem all day and no one would get it so what's the problem with going public?"

"No, no, not the poem, it's the explanation you shouldn't repeat."

"Mom, if no one's interested in the poem, I don't think you have to worry about anybody fighting to find out what it means."

"Thanks for your support. Don't you have some required reading to do?"

This was not how the Girl had intended the conversation to go. There were other things in the poem she admired, and later she even understood that the vampire thing was about how people who did bad things to other people were compelled to do so. It didn't just happen. Nothing just happened. But the Girl had difficulty restarting the conversation.

Whenever she thought she'd worked herself up to the point where she could say, "Mom, I get it: everything is caused," the Singer would pop into her mind, the Singer who emoted seemingly without cause, who could have sung in a dead language or in nonsense syllables and still put across everything she felt and had known and wanted.

As much and as many times as the Girl wanted to go back to her mother to resolve things, it all seemed somehow useless. What she wanted was to be held by her mother as she had been when her mother had come into the room and discovered the Bird. In that moment, the Girl had had everything, her mother's warm slender arms around her back and a hand on the Girl's head pressing her into her mother's shoulder where there was just enough room to breathe and between the Girl's eyes and the base her skull was the song that ran out of the Singer and through the Bird.

But now, thinking on the moment, the Singer she imagined as the source of the Bird's pleading song left her feeling as if there was no use talking to her mother. The most brilliant words were stupid and her words weren't even as brilliant as her mother's that had to be explained, and explanations were stupid and so on and so on. It was much easier to remember and to be lost in the song and so that is where she remained, even through her required reading.

***

Before the Author learned to tell a story that could be sold to many people, and after her husband the Scientist lost his job, he became desperate to find work. It seemed unwise to him to rely on his wife selling a book as a good source of income. He loved her work but had stopped trying to tell people about it because they would become unconscious and that would bring the conversation to a close. As you have probably guessed, he spent a lot of time with his own thoughts, which was ironic given the nature of his research.

The thrust of his research had begun years ago. There had been an incident that made him certain he could find a way to link people into one another's conscious minds, if not the subconscious. It was all part of a clinical trial where he and his wife had met. She had volunteered to be a test subject for a study on psychotropic, or psychedelic, drugs, depending on how you pronounce it.

He just happened to walk into the area where she was being interviewed when the screening device began to ask the same question over and over. She was about to walk out before he cut off the machine and began conducting the interview himself.

The sound of her voice took him away from the content of her answers. What she said was clear enough to him. She did seem to use many words for things he thought of as being easier to describe, and though she was not speaking loudly, there was a certain stream of force to her words. It enthralled him. He was sure he'd heard nothing like it. It was perhaps the one thing he'd encountered since childhood for which he had no point of reference but that nonetheless made him happy.

Towards the end of the interview, he realized his speaking had not caused her to fall asleep, that she had not so much as yawned. He became so nervous with happiness that he had to enter codes more than once to process the interview. Despite his agitation, the woman thought he was now more real and relaxed than when he calmly took over the interview from the device. She hoped that she'd had something to do with that.

As for the actual experiment, she'd had psychotropics before and found the idea of being paid to take them quite attractive. She wondered what he would be like on mushrooms. Perhaps it would open his more human side up to the codes he knew and the codes would be changed.

She didn't take all of the drugs the experimenters gave her and managed to smuggle what she saved past the guards and into the control area where the Scientist sat, somewhat isolated at his workstation.

"Have you had any of this Bliss Garden brand?"

Her voice caught everyone's attention. Hardly anyone there communicated by speaking and she was not authorized to be there in any event. She set the container of relief drink down on the area of his desk where she thought he would put food from home or personal items, though she couldn't imagine him with either. She smiled at him as no one else had, as if the two of them had a history of the most intimate communication.

He was in an unnatural state. Little else mattered to him beyond the sound of her voice. For instance, it barely registered to him that the container she gave him was open. Even the Bliss Garden, the only relief drink dispensed in his area for all of the years he'd been there, seemed new in her hands.

***

The study was well under way when he began to notice a distinct change in his perception. He was watching himself conducting the interview with the Author. But instead of answering the questions, she was laughing approvingly and pointing to a set of wings growing out of his back.

He didn't know what to make of her laughter or his wings. He was wholly focused on the sensation that he was seeing the world from inside the woman's mind. This new perspective excited him so, he had the urge to run out of the facility and re-experience all the books of fiction and poetry he'd avoided in school, every piece of artwork, music, film, and dance he'd ever had to screen. He managed to fight that urge because it might cost him his job. At the same time, the thought of getting paid for doing science became more absurd by the moment.

Everything in his head was now madly spinning around the desire to exchange what was in him with someone else, to trade who he was with another person and simultaneously to know that experience through what he had always thought was his own consciousness.

The very idea of being able to engage people without boring them senseless made him almost immobile with a strange joy. The loneliness that had tracked him like a hound, that he had been trying to deny since childhood, felt too close to ignore. It almost had a face, a presence he could grasp and dispatch.

***

The Author and the Scientist got together after the experiment. They met at a public music machine event. The opening comedy act was so amazingly lifelike that some folks didn't laugh when it began dismembering itself and making jokes about the pain. The performer then opened its chest, pulled out the pulsing equivalent of its heart, and pointed to a patron in the front circle who was laughing almost to the point of tears.

"Looks like you could use one these," the act said, and tried to give the organ to the person in the front who was now convulsed with laughter.

But not everyone was laughing. There were, in fact, enough twinges of sadness throughout the crowd to register with Review Services. People actually tried to hack the names of the employees who had authored the creature. In fact, there were so many serious and sophisticated hacks into the system, the authorities had difficulty trying to fine people for illegal access.

Even the Scientist was tempted to look up the names of those employees, as he was so taken aback by the detailed "biology" of the stagecraft.

"It was almost like the mind meld of video work," he said with as much admiration as his affectless voice would allow.

"No, no," laughed the Author. "Video is just straight narcotic, opiate. This sort of stagecraft is way more psychedelic, like the Bliss Garden."

"Bliss Garden?" he said, utterly puzzled.

It dawned on her, or actually hit her like a freight train, that he'd somehow experienced the psychedelics she'd slipped into his drink without realizing it was drugs that had altered his consciousness. When he'd first told her about seeing the wings on his back, she'd just smiled and he smiled and she put her head to his. They'd fallen into kissing and made love. Now, she realized how completely she understood him. She even knew his blind spots and had a hint of how large those blind spots had grown in the vacuum of his social interactions.

"Yes my dearest," she almost cooed as she grasped his hand, "Where do you think your wings came from?"

He sat back without releasing her hand, but was lost in what was almost a full-blown flashback. The hallucinations had not been what occupied him at the time and, somehow, had not fully registered as having been chemically induced. It was the connection he'd felt most deeply. Her laughter at his wings had had no content or affect beyond the melody of her voice, and even that had been swallowed by the experience of being in another person's mind and in his own all at once.

She mistook the look of wonder on his face as one of humiliation and, at that moment, decided the two of them would never do psychedelics together again. He was precious to her. There would be time enough later to shore up his fragilities.

They eventually got married and pregnant. The pregnancy started out fine, but the closer they came to delivery, the more anxious the Author became. Days before the due date, she contacted her old supplier and procured some psychedelics that had generally been good for relieving anxiety. She debated whether to take them before the delivery or to take them the day of. But the days before were filled with preparation, so she waited.

Most of the time, she had dropped acid in comfortable, controlled situations that had already gone a long way toward reducing anxiety. The new experience of birthing a child was one that made her feel acutely anxious—this despite all the encouragement and instruction she and the Scientist had received from the one midwife they could find, a kind but positively ancient (she still had a functioning phone and a driver's license) woman.

The Author dropped the acid on the day she was sure she would deliver, taking slightly more than she had planned but a bit less than usual. It was the contractions that most concerned her and that she most meditated upon at first, despite herself. When the medical information says to anticipate pain, you know it's going to hurt, but the actual experience of pain, the specifics of it, you may not know until the actual event, and so it was for her with childbirth.

The Midwife thought the Author's breathing was quite shallow and encouraged her to take deeper breaths. The acid had begun to take hold and, to the Author, it seemed as though she was already inhaling and exhaling vast oceans of air, more than any human had a right to. For a moment, she feared there might not be enough air left for others in the room there to assist with the birth. Nonetheless, she had a great deal of trust in the very dark woman with the very deep folds of skin beneath her eyes, and if the woman requested hurricane strength breathing, then a hurricane it would be. The Midwife's approval of the increased breathing gave the Author such a feeling of warmth and accomplishment that she almost forgot about the contractions and the fact that her body, the bones in her pelvis, would soon open wide enough to let another person, albeit a small one, through.

Imagining what the baby would be like, she found herself squatting in a pool of blue light. There with her in the blue was the Midwife, and her husband the Scientist, doing as they had done in the birthing room. In the darkness, she could see musical instruments.

This must be a stage, she thought, and had the sudden urge to look behind her to see if there were seats where the audience used to sit. That was wrong she thought. It was not where the audience used to be seated but would be seated. Clearly, a performance was about to take place. The instruments and the devices into which people would speak (sing?) were shiny and in place, ready to go. In fact, someone was already singing. Was she practicing? Yes, she was warming up, a woman's voice but sometimes sounding like a girl.

"This is the first birth in thirty-five years where I haven't known the gender and god knows what else about the child before it came," said the Midwife, both happy and nostalgic. "But it feels like a girl. Anyway, it's time to push."

***

The pressure to create a normal story was very different from the pressure the Author had felt when it came time to give birth. There was no pleasure woven into the fear. The surges of anxiety around the story never came with unexplained laughter as they had when she carried the child.

Though, the economic anxiety and pressure of her husband being out of work did not worry her as much or concern her in the same way as the lack of anything between the two of them. It wasn't uncommon for couples to feel a bit at sea once a child came along. But this was more troubling.

She'd first noticed it right after the birth. He had been talking enthusiastically about what it would be like to be at home with the baby. But her mind drifted to what she'd seen and where she'd been for a good chunk of her labor. Pieces of what he'd said "on stage" began to replace what he was saying at the moment, and she couldn't untangle the sentences he was speaking now from what he'd said while she was high and delivering.

He noticed the sad and frustrated look on her face and his enthusiasm flagged. She hadn't seen that look on his face since he'd entered the room to fix the interview device. She hoped he would not ask her to react in any way to what he'd just said because she had no idea what he'd just said.

He grasped her hand, but his expression was blank, and she realized that affectless mask was what he wore to hide the hurt of almost never being heard. She swore to herself then that she would never take another hit of acid no matter how anxious she became. She kept her promise she made to herself, even though there were times when she was certain that a good dose of something psychoactive would have helped the story and or the marriage. Then she would realize there was no potion for either.

Whenever she tried to focus on creating a story that could sell and, thereby, lift them from the poverty that seemed otherwise certain, she drifted inexorably to thinking about ways to get back to where she and the Scientist had been when he had taken over the interview. Time was not on her side, but she could not help returning to videos with discussions about modifications one could make that would recapture what had been lost in a relationship or that would at least alter your perception of the other person in your relationship.

Naturally, some of these modifications were failures. The Author stumbled upon a piece from an anonymous woman who claimed that she had been a singing star, that screeners would recognize her singing voice even coming from a cheap device.

This singing star had tried to alter her perception of her husband, who happened to be in business with her. She had gotten
into the habit of perception-alterations because her husband
was abusive, so abusive, in fact, that he had forbidden her to
change the way she perceived him. In short, he wanted her
to be fully and utterly aware of what he was doing, who was
"in charge."

None of this was apparent to the fan base or even the patrons.
The singer noted the pain and solace she experienced from the
isolation of her private life and the exhilaration of her "stage"
life, seeing people go wild over the group's holograms with her
voice and image at the tip of the spear.

Somehow, she managed to get away long enough to get to a
clinic where she could have the alterations to her perceptions
done. It was doubly difficult to find a place that would be discreet. The "bad" publicity would have added to their fan base,
but it would also have made her personal life worse. Things got
worse anyway.

Perhaps the practitioners were quacks. Perhaps the sort of
alterations she sought didn't really exist. Whatever the case,
her perceptions of her husband were in no way softened by the
alterations, but rather intensified. His jokes about her looks,
her "mistakes" during the act, how she owed all of her fame to
his management—all of these things seemed both more petty
and more vicious. Worse, she could feel the threats coming,
sometimes long before he actually spoke. This sensitivity gave
time a hallucinatory feel that made it drag and yet, somehow,
seemed to shorten the periods between insults and threats.

Her reaction, fueled by the feelings of disappointment and
betrayal, was a disgust she could not hide. He took it as a sign of
defiance and became more violent until the physical alterations

wouldn't hold and, finally, her voice failed her. The Author had found her story.

2. The Antecedent Blues or The Water This Time

There was a woman who loved to sing and dance whose parents left her to grow up with her grandmother in a quiet town where her singing and dancing drew attention, good and bad. People who liked and disliked the dancing said it reminded them of what they'd seen and heard or what other people had said they'd seen and heard in the much bigger city of Strummale, or Mailstrumville, depending on how you pronounce it, where things were much wilder.

The woman made plans to leave for the bigger city. Perhaps she would find fame and fortune there. Perhaps one of her parents would show up and she could ask where the hell they'd been. The grandmother was lukewarm on the woman going to the city. She thought the woman had extraordinary talent but also knew show business was a tough nut to crack.

The grandmother had in fact once tried to make it singing and dancing and had ended up being the "Singing Weather Girl," on local radio, and then the "All Singing, All Dancing Weather Girl," on the old screens you could hold or set on the table. She was a bit stiff and hoarse from all the singing and dancing, but the grandmother still paid what some would call an inordinate amount of attention to weather patterns and forecast and had taken to warning people whenever she could about how the temperature of the planet was rising and the problems that would follow as night follows day.

But, every time she brought it up, the older people couldn't help but remember how beautiful her voice had been on the radio and screen, and the content of what she said was crowded

out by their memories. The younger people who had no knowledge or memory of radios or the earlier plain, flat, external
screens were confused by the dissonance between the memories
as described by others and what the Grandmother said. Thus
the content of her warnings sank like a stone in the ocean
at night.

The woman as a girl was the only person who ever really
heard what the Grandmother said, and even that was for a particular and short-lived time. They talked about simple things
when the woman was younger and deeper things as she grew.

When the Girl had been very young, the Grandmother
would sing and recite things she had learned from her father
who had learned the songs from his great-great grandfather
who had been a Gandy Dancer, back in the days when transports ran on tracks.

> Up and down the road I go
> Skippin' and a dodgin' forty fo'
> Hey man, can't you line it
> Hey man, won't you line it

The Girl laughed herself silly and it took awhile for the
Grandmother to realize that the mere sound of her voice in
recitation was what caused the infant to laugh. By the time the
Girl learned to speak, she and the Grandmother sang.

> If you were lost to me would I cry
> Enough to roll the deepest river
> Drown a mountain in the sky

As the Girl grew, she learned that everyone has a mother and
father and began to ask about hers. Why weren't they around?
The Grandmother had no good answers or produced different

slices of answers for the same question no matter how many times it was asked. The parents had to go away. They didn't get along. They had only small things in common. They broke up shortly after the Girl was born. They were singers whose voices brought them together and then took them in opposite directions when money entered the equation.

This frustrated the Girl. The Grandmother would begin singing when she saw the Girl's frustration, singing deeper, singing as though the Girl was not there or not there alone but listening along with the whole world, and the presence or seeming presence of so many enraptured souls soothed the Girl's frustration and made the grandmother's voice seem like the biggest, softest place that could ever be.

On the day the woman was scheduled to leave for the big city, the Grandmother became aware of an approaching storm and begged the woman to stay and ride it out in the shelter she and her now dead partner had built. The woman almost relented. But her bags were packed and it was a gorgeous, though amazingly humid, day and the thought of riding the transport in air-conditioned comfort (her grandmother had air conditioning but rarely used it and never set it any lower than 80 Fahrenheit) proved too big a temptation, and so the woman took off.

The storm didn't strike as you might have expected, at the point in the story where the woman got on the transport and was waving goodbye to her sadly quiet Grandmother who sang to her even though she could not be heard through the transport glass and certainly thought it would be the last time she'd see her granddaughter. The storm did hit just as the woman reached Strummale or Mailstrumville.

She was dismayed and confused to see huge swaths of vacant land and half repaired damage all over the city from what must have been previous storms as she gazed out the transport window. The past and present storms merged in her mind with the rubble and the half repairs.

Thunder rattled windows and shook the ground. Multiple bolts of lightning struck near and far and the already nervous driver leapt screaming from the vehicle as it plunged into a crater that may have been a sinkhole or the site of a controlled exploded ordinance or the basement of a very small illegally constructed building. Whatever it was, it was big enough to consume the entire section of transport with the rest of the people who were going to, near, or past the cheap hotel she had booked for herself.

The wind piled debris above them, closing them off from the storm and daylight such as it was. The darker it got, the more frightened and panicked everyone became, including the woman. She could see almost nothing now but her Grandmother standing near the transport, singing as it pulled away, and though she could not hear her Grandmother, she knew what she was singing.

and like a river it's gonna flow
like love in sunlight can't help but grow

It had seemed sad but mostly quaint to see her Grandmother singing out loud to someone who could not hear her through the thick glass of the transport. It had brought a strange smile to the woman's face as the Grandmother and the town disappeared. But now, with the daylight being swallowed, the full weight of that moment felt like another storm.

Oxygen was becoming a precious commodity in the sunken transport. Nonetheless, the woman's sadness propelled her singing voice so that the sheer volume of it brought a level of discomfort that caused others onboard to try to wrestle her to the ground and cover her mouth. But they were weak from the rising heat and diminished air and were not fired with memories of a Grandmother singing and disappearing in the distance. So the woman was able to wrestle free and continued to belt out the song like someone possessed of the Holy Ghost or Orishas (depending on how you pronounce it), drawing the oxygen out of the small darkening space.

Enough to roll the deepest river
Drown a mountain in the sky

***

Weaker, twenty-first century-type storms were still rocking the area when the first rescue flights were sent. The machines were, of course, flown by inmates who could be persuaded to do so. One prisoner pilot who had gotten his privileges by singing and playing guitar thought he might have been hallucinating (could it have been the pain from the device strapped to his head to control the machine?) when his listening device fed him what sounded like singing. Did he know that song or was it just one of those songs that sounded like a song you thought you knew even though you'd never heard it before?

A probe confirmed there was life at the site of the singing. He sent for machines to probe the area. They were flown in quickly. Crews drilled air holes into the debris and began to remove it layer by layer. Nat thought the rescue of one person would surely move up his release date. When he discovered a transport full of people and got the lowdown on the singing, he could see total freedom on the horizon.

Acting against the orders issued during his training, Nat, the musical prisoner pilot, landed the flying device. The other crew member inmates were taken aback by Nat's presence, by his going against orders to land the vehicle. Some, mostly the white people, thought he was another crazy black inmate and gave him lots of personal space.

There were levels of chaos swirling in Nat that had pushed or allowed him to land. One was created by the storm itself. The training that was to enable him to ignore it was as shoddy as any of the training he'd received.

The other source of chaos was more tinged with hope. That, of course, came from the Singer. Fragmented and tangential to all of that was a story in his head—a story that must have come from an old external screen or a grandparent. The parts of the story he could recall made him want to be the first person the Singer saw when she emerged from the wreck. But, when daylight touched the Singer's eyes, the sky was what she saw, and it lifted her past the tears she'd shed thinking of her Grandmother.

Even in her sweaty disheveled state, or because of her sweaty disheveled state, the Singer was beautiful. She looked like she had barely escaped from deep inside a burning building or had just swum away from a vehicle that had crashed in the water or had done something else that demanded every ounce of blood, will, and focus to accomplish. Nat realized that was what he'd heard in her voice when he'd been flying over the wreckage of the transport—a desperation he'd thought belonged to him alone. It was the echo of that desperation in her voice that had made the unfamiliar song seem familiar and made him want to be with her and her music.

People were offering the Singer food, drink, and light wraps. She took the aid, smiling and thanking the people, all the while looking up. It wasn't until Nat spoke that she looked at anyone for any length of time.

"I've heard that song. What was that you were singing?"

"You couldn't have heard it before. But that's a wonderful compliment and I'll be sure to tell my grandmother."

She felt the need to sit down, to gather herself. Her sweat dried and cooled her even through the light wraps. Time began to pass again. She could feel her own weight. She looked up just in time to see police hog tie Nat and all but throw him into a transport. Then she realized she and Nat were some of the very few dark-skinned people in the area and that she had been the only dark person on the transport.

***

The first part of the story that brought the Singer a bit of celebrity was that one of her fellow passengers had blood dripping from one ear. It had been damaged by the volume of the song the Singer sang in the transport. The person with the damaged ear wanted to take the Singer to court until the other passengers vehemently protested. What was one impaired ear compared to them all dying slowly and horribly buried beneath rubble? That surely would have been the outcome had the Singer not sang so loudly.

Reporters began to hound the Singer. She decided to use one of her Grandmother's names and told them she was Tina. She repeatedly asked reporters if they knew the prisoner who had heard her singing from beneath the rubble.

***

Tina's notoriety increased when they found the prisoner. The sight of him, knowing he was not dead, gave her a rush of relief. She embraced him even though his clothes were inexplicably damp.

She learned his name was Nat. Inevitably, someone suggested they form the Nat and Tina Turner Revue, but also suggested that, unlike his namesake, Nat should not murder white men, women, or children in the course of Black Liberation. Nearly every media outlet suggested they could, like Ike and Tina Turner, "make a killing with their music." Many people thought that was a stupid thing to say even when they wrote it. But the media is filled with people paid to say stupid things, and this was one of those stupid things that spread like the flu.

Their high profiles and public curiosity actually gave Nat and Tina enough cover to circumvent the law and perform live without the usual bureaucratic nightmare of meeting virtually impossible qualifications. Even so, the Recording Institute for Public Safety (RIPS) was just biding its time before intervening. Their legal and public persuasion people decided their reputations could, as usual, use a little boost. So, they would let Nat and Tina go without hologram agreements for at least a little longer. The musical duo did keep up appearances by appearing in news grams, but for free, and as preludes to live performances.

Those performances, all of course in small, low-tech venues, were packed. Everyone wanted to hear the woman who managed to sing her way out of what should have been her grave. Some even thought they wanted to hear a voice that could damage their ears. What they got was blues updated by the Revue with a group of musicians that were drawn to Nat and

Tina. Every show ended with an a cappella version of "River Deep, Mountain High." Many in the audience heard things they'd never heard before, never knew they could hear, things they didn't know were there to be heard.

The most affected members of the audience were unable to speak or move for a few moments after she was done. The silence after her sound fell out of time. A warm clear gap filled the listeners' heads. After the show, they would sit at home in the quietest rooms they could find for unspecified moments. They would, at first unintentionally, disrupt work sites by sitting still. They began to congregate and create more serious disruptions.

***

Tina danced provocatively to every number except the last one, and that is one of the things that made it Nat's favorite besides the fact that it reminded him of meeting her, seeing her emerge from the jaws of death like Venus the Warrior.

After a practice session that had left everyone sweating, the two of them had wandered off, talking. Nat asked her about her dancing during the show. Didn't she think it was a distraction? Wasn't it too much of a contrast with the last and most powerful number?

"There's all kinds of power, don't you think?" she said, noticing they were alone. She gyrated slowly towards him and then away. He followed her.

***

A Producer saw the smiling couple on video that was passed to him on the company implant from an underpartner desperate to keep her job, and so discreetly slipped the intel through her home implant. The Producer fired her even though he instantly recognized the couple as being marketable. He would have to find some way to bring them into his stable.

He was used to having leverage, but what kind of leverage could he manage with an ex-con and this woman who had survived an incredible crash by singing loud enough to be heard through collapsed buildings? It would have to be through the prisoner and the prison system, somehow. Having barely escaped serving time himself, the Producer had some familiarity with how things worked versus how things were supposed to work.

He was able to persuade prison officials to rescind some of the musical prisoner's freedom, and Nat and Tina found themselves in the Producer's office with two linked agreements on portable parchment before them. One cut Nat free of prison, sort of. The other made the Nat and Tina Turner Revue the virtual property of the Producer for one year and gave them a huge bonus for signing both parchments. The fact that it was only a year, that it took prison out of the picture for Nat and gave them a huge bonus, led Nat and Tina to sign.

"When do we hit the studio?" Nat asked with a slightly forced smile after his biometrics scanned through the last agreement.

"I just need her, I just need her to sing the song," the Producer said without looking up. "But she's got to sing it perfectly."

"I've been singing it since before I knew what it meant," said Tina, her smile fading as the last word left her. "Nobody else can touch it. I've rehearsed the hell—"

"You," the Producer said looking at Nat, "can rest up while she records."

***

After much back and forth, Tina arrived without Nat at the Producer's lair to record the song. The Producer's ideas seemed both strange and right to her. With most recordings, errors were corrected with the hologram. The Producer, however, made "live" corrections, whole corrections, at least for a while. When even the slightest thing went wrong, all of the musicians—she had never been in a room with so many: dozens of people with real wooden and metal instruments—would play the whole song from the beginning through to the end.

The sound he was able to garner from the musicians was such that she wondered why he bothered with grams. Surely, he had the wealth and clout to go live with what could only be described as a towering vortex of sound. It swelled and ebbed like a story even when there was no singing, and when there was singing, the sound became a beast with wings.

She was so fascinated by the process that it took her a while to notice that her voice was slowly deteriorating from the long, relentless days of singing. When she pointed this out to the Producer, the room fell silent. Most of the people in the room had worked with him before and dreaded his reaction.

It began with him banging his fist on the recording interface and ripping the monitor nodes from his scalp. His assistant was used to the small splatters of blood that came with this as the Producer insisted on using the older, more primitive nodes.

"You think he was in prison when he was sent out to rescue you, is that what you think?" the Producer shouted as his pale face flushed with blood. "I can send his black ass to *prison*, do you hear me? Old Testament style, no fucking holds barred sho'nuff prison. You want him in a game complex, is that what you want? Because that's where he's going if you think you're going to fuck me over. You signed a contract! I'm spending money, you spend your voice!"

No one dared speak or move for a few moments. The Singer flashed back to her Grandmother singing an old song. Then she closed her eyes and swallowed her tears.

***

It was weeks before she saw Nat again. She could barely speak. Her eyes were vacant and rimmed by puffy skin. The Producer had arranged a private transport. The door stood open as passersby stared at them holding one another, rocking slowly.

***

Tina did not listen to vocal music for some time after her sessions with the Producer. As her voice began to heal, she told Nat the story of the recording: about the threats and how, towards the end, she was actually happy that the Producer barely spoke to her, how raw her throat was and that it only worked with sample correction, how the Producer insisted that she supplement the hologram with her live voice even though it was clear that the gram would be mostly sample. She'd been run ragged.

On the rare evenings she had not gone straight to bed after the sessions, she'd tried to program things to watch. No matter what she programmed, there was always a short gram on a prototype prison where the inmates fought modified versions of one another for entertainment—whose entertainment she was unsure. But the point was made.

Nat was almost lost in remorse. While she was gone, he dreamt of her singing beneath the rubble of the storm. But, in the dream, the sound would fade just as he got close. He had to fight with the Warden to get permission to dig, all the while insisting there was someone there. But when the site was clear, there was only an empty transport in a cavernous hole.

***

"I was still glowing, so happy to not be dead in that hellhole without air, that I would have agreed to anything. If there's a next time."

***

"The only thing I wanted to hear was your voice pushing through the storm and all the junk that had piled up."

***

"He was the mirror image of you, to say nothing of my grandmother. She could hear me in her sleep."

***

"I can't remember anything I dreamed while you were gone."

***

The gram of Tina singing "River Deep, Mountain High" from the Producer's sessions was a mammoth success. The final version even had Nat fixed into it post-production, and he looked quite natural, none of the usual ashen skin of likenesses. Nat and Tina imagined the Producer must have spent a small fortune for it.

Ironically, the gram played venues for high-end private affairs where those who, like Nat, had re-entered society were scanned and questioned before they were allowed in. The fact that the holograms played at these venues gave the real Nat and Tina even more cover to play live.

Still, the experience with the Producer haunted them. Tina wrote about it to try to purge it from her gut. Nat tried not to blame himself for the way the Producer treated Tina. But he had only been out of prison a short time before the Producer made his "offer" and brought back the feeling of being incarcerated, not for Nat himself, but, he feared, for someone he loved. It felt like prison was a virus he had somehow managed to pass on to Tina.

***

Prison was where Nat had learned a lot of things, including the details of slavery in the US. Discovering that had been like discovering the name, cause, and details of a low-grade fever he'd inherited and had all his life. Being of African descent, the subject was one he'd heard mentioned since he was a child. It was made most clear to him when his seventh or eighth grade class actually had the same teacher for six consecutive months in what he now realized was a history class (though he couldn't recall the official name).

As with most of their teachers, the class was desperate to know what she did for a living outside of the classroom, and how and if they could learn whatever she knew that earned her money. They saw that as the most pragmatic use of their time, though few of them had any idea what the word pragmatic meant.

The woman had been trained as a musician. She claimed to play a type of music where only some of it was planned or written down. The most important parts were made up by the musicians based on how well they listened to one another and on their personalities and life experiences. This seemed funny and crazy to him and his classmates. Music, like writing and movies, was mostly the work of machines. None of them had heard of any of the people the woman said were her role models. Some thought she was making a joke, perhaps even making fun of them even after she snuck her instrument, a "trumpet," into the classroom. It had three moving parts on it she called valves. She stuck something into the opening (she called it the "bell") of the thing where the sound came out so that it wouldn't be so loud.

He could not recall the name of anything she played, but whenever he remembered her playing, whatever room he was in dissolved with the sound. He remembered how he couldn't wait for the next note but felt that he knew what was coming. The experience and what the woman had told the class about it split his head open. He thought what he heard was something dark that she alone had created, something that could only be created alone. At the same time, he could not imagine that what she played had not been touched and built up by many people before her. It seemed impossible for one person to have created what felt like a huge building, a skyscraper of sound. It seemed equally unlikely that it ever occupied space where they were, a dim low ceiling of a room, in a building where the hallways had even less light and the only movement allowed was from room to room. The sound she made with her eyes closed was its own light.

A mere few days after he'd experienced the music, it troubled him that he had no idea how such people could have existed in the numbers necessary to create the sound his teacher had played for them. Who could these now dead musicians have been? Almost nothing he'd been taught or had screened over the years supported what the woman, teacher, musician had said or done. It left him skeptical of his own experience.

It wasn't until years later that Nat realized how deep and true the woman's lessons had been. He still had tattered "magazines" of real paper she'd given him. She'd handed them to him with a sad, pleading smile.

"I hope you can give these a good home," she'd said one day after school.

She couldn't tell him it was the last time he'd see her. She'd learned her sleep unit had been probed and it would not be wise for her to return to it.

The magazines had articles about her heroes—Billie Holiday, Pops Armstrong, Bird, Duke, Miles, Sarah, Mingus, Sun Ra, Cecil, on and on. There was one, Max Roach, who had a group of songs that were all linked together by an idea, the enslavement of people of African descent in the US by primarily wealthy white people in Europe and the Americas, and the aftermath of that enslavement. Strangely, the work never mentioned white people as such. Clearly, the overseers and slaveowners had been white. But that word didn't surface. The authors assumed their audience had a modicum of knowledge about who had dragged whom in chains across the ocean in the bottoms of rat-infested, corpse-riddled boats.

Nat noticed that a lot while he was looking up stuff about the Max Roach record. If you didn't do the research—and why would you?—it seemed that the racism used to excuse slavery was a thing that just happened, like a disease that afflicted you most likely if you had dark skin, and though the phrase "free labor" was prevalent throughout the various texts, the serious economic drivers and outcomes were rarely probed in depth. You could almost conclude it was an affliction with no human cause.

When Nat's research on the Max Roach record corroborated what the teacher had said about slavery, many things fell into place. He could see or at least imagine a vague outline of the group of people needed to create music that could drive everything else from the mind, music whose foundation was a cathartic shout—"make me wanna holla" one text pro-claimed—wrapped in a moan.

Jazz became an obsession, albeit a latent one. It took him a while to realize it wasn't exactly safe to discuss his findings in public. Fortunately, the police didn't frequent his neck of the woods, or they had much bigger fish to fry than subversive cultural material. He exhausted video references for the music pretty quickly, and though his curiosity was great, his need to find a way to make a living was greater.

One day, he began toying with the bizarre idea that he could earn money playing music in drug emporiums. It would be a way to directly engage the roots of jazz, the antecedent blues. The police rarely showed up at these places. The patrons were engaged in legal activity and were often dead to the world in any event.

He found the plans for a guitar at some underground site with temporary implants that seemed barely clean and cajoled some gangster printer into making the instrument. Why a guitar? It could play chords as well as the usual single notes and yet, unlike a piano, was cheap, portable, and low mainte-nance, and, unlike a violin was easier to play and keep tuned. It could play jazz and it could play popular music. He'd seen lots of pop musicians from the old days playing guitar even as the video avails were dwindling. He'd also seen pictures of a player named Charlie Christian, a guitarist. He'd never heard Christian's playing, but imagined it was different than the wild gyrations and feedback he screened from the pop musicians.

Nat got a job running the cleaning machines at a particu-larly grungy emporium called the Veiled Woman. He chose it because even with a lot of people talking all at once, the place sounded quiet. It had obviously been used for something else at some point in time. It was run by a guy who always wore the same greasy blue jacket with the initials LJ on the front. Though all the "clients" called him LJ, he insisted Nat call him "Proprietor."

The Proprietor's machines sat on a wide raised part of the floor. Nat thought this was unique and clever, a good way to keep an eye on what was going on in the tattered seats that faced the raised area. The large area that overhung the seats was a total mystery, as were the seats in small raised pockets off to the side. Why have places where it would be hard for the Proprietor to see what was going on without swiveling around? Who could afford to screen all that area, to say nothing of cleaning it?

The Proprietor just chuckled when Nat brought this up to him one day when things were slow with only about a hundred people in the chairs.

"You're a good one, you are," smiled the Proprietor.

Once he had some months of practice under his belt, Nat felt confident enough to ask about playing music for pay in addition to cleaning.

Referring to the drug users, the Proprietor snorted, "They've got their own music."

"This will come close to breaking the law," Nat almost whispered. "It will attract a whole new group of people. Some might not be addicts, just users."

LJ tried not to show excitement. How was it that this youngster could come to him offering the holy grail of emporiums, to bring users among the addicts? Could it be real? LJ smiled, realizing he had nothing to lose.

It took some weeks before word got out that you could hear a live musician at the Veiled Woman. The crowds began to grow slowly and virtually none of the new clientele threw up on themselves or passed out in a puddle of their own urine. The Proprietor was able to hire a young woman to clean when Nat was onstage, where he began to spend most of his time.

It's inevitable that a place that attracts people who use and abuse drugs is frequented by a fair amount of artists in general and musicians in particular. The VW was no different. There were even musicians or ex-musicians who admitted, albeit cryptically, that they had experience with the guitar. Some even admitted to owning an instrument themselves and praised Nat for being brave enough to go "public" even if it was in a place the authorities were unlikely to disturb. One particularly wizened woman whose spine curved over her thin straight legs and reminded Nat of a question mark was still agile enough to roll on her back while playing the guitar, could play the instrument behind her head and behind her back and pluck solos with her teeth.

She also had theories about why music sounded different north of the Caribbean, how one set of white people had sent families to take over the land from the people they found there versus how another group of whites had sent mostly soldiers, young men who would be away from "home" for years.

"Sex. Everything's different when you know the sex in the music," she said at the end of her lectures on the Caribbean Divide in the music.

Though he could speculate on the meaning of this, he decided it was not as important as learning as much music from her as he could in the time she had left on the planet.

There was another deadline pressure building slowly that was wholly unknown and perhaps unknowable as far as Nat and millions like him were concerned. Nat saw the tip of the iceberg on a battered, half-broken hand screen the Old Woman had scammed from a desperate addict. She had dropped the screen rushing to the latrine. It began a story about a heretofore unemployed Scientist who had found a way to make a living by curing mostly rich people of the earworm problem from the odd pink bird. The Scientist cured the earworm by putting those who had it into a deeper sleep than they had had since childhood. The earworm left by the odd pink bird began to fade with the first treatment. By the third session of deeply induced sleep, their minds were clear of the obnoxious repeated sound.

"Good for them," Nat thought, as the Old Woman returned, looking relieved.

What Nat didn't know, the part of the story that was developing far below the screens, was what else the Scientist was doing with the people he cured. He was scanning their brains to try to understand, as any appropriately curious person would, why these particular people had been susceptible to the earworm in the first place.

This is where the news story became odd. In fact, it didn't seem quite like a news story. He couldn't quite place it.

". . . and this is where the findings differ. Researcher Dimear spoke at length on his personal memories of people performing music onstage aided only by mechanical amplification and sometimes not even that."

"What one recalls is the lack of power and effectiveness of the so-called live performances versus . . ."

Here, the screen failed for moment. Then there was another media person speaking.

". . . modern tools that Ellington or Mozart would not only have praised but would have used themselves. It would have let them open up deeper parts of their work. I almost laughed when these folks claimed some connection between the earworm and live music . . ."

The Old Woman put her hand on his head. "Get off that damn screen, fool. Ain't nothin' but shit on there."

"But you finagled your way into one."

"I'm old. They cain't change me. You want to wind up with them wires in your head so you cain't never turn it off or you want to make some music? You let me know."

***

Nat was able to persuade the Old Woman to perform with him, much to the delight of the users, the addicts, and, as the crowd grew, total nonusers. The addicts were in fact being crowded out even as Nat and the Old Woman performed songs of the great Tommy Johnson, whose repertoire she'd been reluctant to cover given the audience's substance abuse.

"What you wanna learn that shit for? He was just like these fools we play for."

> Cryin' mama, mama mama
> Know canned heat killin' me . . .
> If canned heat don't kill me
> I won't never die

With Nat going full time to performance, LJ made the Girl who was a part-time cleaner a full-time cleaner and increased everyone's pay. This proved useful in paying for the fines and food and uniforms when the authorities arrived and took the performers to jail for unlicensed live performance.

Nat had been only vaguely aware of the laws designed to keep things a certain way. The way his lawyer eventually explained, the "Safe Distance" statute was that the world was becoming more crowded and so it didn't do to excite large crowds of people. Live music, especially live "popular" music derived from the blues, tended to get people excited, unlike even with the most spectacular events and specials. Very large crowds could walk away from holograms and go relatively quietly into the night.

None of it really made any sense to Nat. He'd known all along that he was doing something illegal or at least close to being illegal. But he had no clear idea why it was illegal and the lawyer's explanation did little to clear that up. People who had come to hear him and the Old Woman were moved by the music of Robert Johnson, Blind Lemon Jefferson, and Charlie Patton, and, as crowds had done centuries ago, synchronized their movements to the music, somewhat akin to the way performers did in holograms these days. But no one was overly excited. In fact, the addicts became, if anything, more contemplative, if one can use that term to describe people whose mental states didn't allow much bladder control.

The non-addicts did tend to get a bit loud, the older ones shouting requests and the younger ones clapping and stomping to the beat. But it was only a little wild, and the fact that it had gone on for some months had led Nat to believe that it would go on as long as LJ opened the doors and made sure the addicts used designated lavatories. LJ even moved his observation booth from the raised floor area and gave it over completely to Nat and the Old Woman.

Nat had felt especially good about the news gram pick-ups. This, he thought, would confer legitimacy. What it did was to no longer allow the authorities to ignore them even if they were much lower priority than serious criminal enterprises such as the Urban Food Alliance or the Anti-Poverty Association suspected of hacking and entering bankers' homes and coercing them into all manner of subversion. Even with such goings on, there was still, somehow, news screen time and prosecution resources for an undereducated, mostly self-taught musician playing the work of people who had been but a generation or so removed from the auction block. There was also still plenty of room for him in the prisons.

***

The smell of the prison, the sound and the drained color, all hit Nat at once. There had been one room, a processing room that clearly at one time had been as clean as the medical facilities of the rich. Only the light colors of the walls remained. It was the room where they were inoculated, supposedly, against the hazards of their assigned jobs.

Everything smelled like oil or plastic that was overheated, on the verge of catching fire. There was that and body odor from the inoculations.

Nat began in a cell with six others, one of whom was mentally ill and prone to attack others. The guards would swoop in, grind the glass of the emergency doors with a swift opening, and sedate the prisoner. The sedation would last for a day or so before he attacked someone again. Everyone was nursing a bruise or a cut, sustained mostly at night or just before sunrise and work. Some were so tired from lack of sleep they slept through at least part of the attack.

After a few months, seven, perhaps nine, Nat was moved to a cell with only four people including him. Two more people replaced him in the other cell. There was no mentally ill person in the new cell. There was a person with some power. The Prisoner had no bracelet monitor and his "uniform," though prison issue, was barely distinguishable from regular clothing.

Nat tried to hide the fear and disappointment in his smile as he greeted the Prisoner first and then the others.

"What you scared of?" the Prisoner spoke in a melodious husky voice, probably altered. "Extra work for extra reward. What's the problem?"

During the day, Nat's job was to mix and apply chemicals to scrap plastic, turning it back into its organic components and making oil in the process. No one knew what was happening to the oil, only that a small percentage of it was burned for energy in remote places. The process of converting plastic back into oil produced the burning smell that permeated everything and that no one ever got used to. Scientists whose pensions didn't allow them to retire studied why no one ever got used to it. The research was endless. People had nightmares about the smell and dreams about escaping it.

With the move to the new cell, Nat had an additional and "unofficial" job. Hours before or after the regular shift, the transparent walls of the cell would become gray and opaque. Everyone but the Prisoner would be fixed for temporary blindness and deafness. When they could see and hear again, they would be seated at equipment used to make the drug AT. It had a long, official, technical name no one but scientists used. Everyone else called it AT or "Away Time." The drug and manufacture of the drug were both official and unofficial rewards and punishments.

The inmate Nat replaced had refused to make AT. He'd seen his mother disfigured and killed by the drug. He tried to reason with the Prisoner and authorities. They all stared at him as if he'd not spoken and then pronounced sentence upon him as if he wasn't there. The next day, he was swapped into the cell where Nat had been with the mentally ill attacker.

One of the concessions to prison "security" was that inmates couldn't use the latest devices to produce AT. The somewhat primitive devices they had to work with meant that operators had to wear goggles and gloves. Fumes from the process slipped behind the eyewear they were given. Stinging, tearing eyes helped them stay awake. It was good to be awake, as mistakes, especially creating overly potent mixtures, were punished with stints in regular cells, or worse.

Lack of sleep began to wear on Nat. The days and nights were hard enough to distinguish through the many layers of the prison's glass. He ceased to be self conscious about having to pee and shit in front of whoever was awake when it came time to relieve himself. Some days, the faucet in the cell didn't work and they had to simply rub their hands on their clothing in an attempt to clean them before eating. The worse part of that was if they'd been creating AT or converting plastic and they could not clean their hands properly until the faucets were working again.

Every once in a while, sometimes at night, an inmate would begin trembling uncontrollably, succumbing to the chemicals that he'd inadvertently ingested. It seemed to take the guards forever to arrive. Sometimes, if the afflicted inmate had angered the cell's Prisoner, the guards would be waved off and the suffering would go unattended. Those who could would turn away from the violent shaking. Those in the cell would put their hands over their ears in a vain attempt to avoid the penetrating, guttural cries.

Nat saw this happen to the man with whom he'd been swapped. Right after a meal, the man in the cell where Nat had been began trembling. People turned away from the gut-wrenching convulsions. Nat found himself caught, wanting to turn away but horribly fixated, almost not believing that anyone could tremble so violently. The Prisoner stared as well, but he was angry, hard as rock. Nat finally was able to turn away when the gray-green liquid drained from the shaking man's nose and ears. When the guards arrived to administer to the trembling man, one of the men in the cell waved them off. The Prisoner in Nat's cell finally turned away.

"He's just waved the guards off to get back at me," the Prisoner scoured.

The next day, the man who had had the convulsions was returned to the cell with Nat, the Prisoner, and the three others. There were now five in the four-person cell. The man recovering from the attack slept on the floor. Indeed, for a while, all he did was sleep.

***

Nat was not large when he entered prison. But he began to lose weight and develop a cough. His throat was rough. Another man in the cell noticed him coughing and asked if he could sing. Nat calmly replied yes, turned his face in the dark to cry silently into the foul bedding, and fell into the deepest sleep he'd had in months.

He awoke with the voice of the Old Woman in his head and began to sing along with a Robert Johnson song she'd taught him.

> Got to keep moving, Got to keep moving
> Blues falling down like hail, blues falling down like hail
> Mmm, blues falling down like hail, blues falling down
>   like hail
> And the day keeps on remindin' me, there's a hellhound on
>   my trail

Hellhound on my trail, hellhound on my trail

The man Nat replaced began to stir.

"That's hoodoo music. What you singin' that hoodoo music for?"

Nat had no idea what the man was talking about. But he was very glad the man seemed too weak to get up from the floor, as his face was contorted with fear and anger.

The Prisoner, on the other hand, liked Nat's singing.

"I don't know what you singing. Maybe you know something else to sing."

Nat continued singing Robert Johnson, though he began to recall some Bessie Smith and, later, some Big Maybelle.

Candy,

I call my sugar Candy

The other men in the cell dropped their heads or slumped against the wall.

"Go back to the other stuff about the hound dog or the heart like a rock in the water," the Prisoner quickly demanded.

Nat tried to smile and said he was tired of singing, needed a rest. The Prisoner tried not to show he was angered. Why should some asshole refusing to sing anger him? The Prisoner slept badly and awoke early, and even though he felt horrible and exhausted, he got the other men up to begin processing AT. The man Nat replaced was now able to sit up. But he was still disoriented and the Prisoner didn't bother to assign him a processing station.

Nat's eyes stung from sleeplessness and stung more from the process. He tried to be more careful than usual. One of the other men, an older man, was struggling to stay awake. Nat dared not interrupt his own work to rouse the sleepy man. All he could think to do was sing. A curious song came to him. It was one of the songs he'd had to almost beg the Old Woman to teach him. She said she thought it might have been a prison work song.

Ain't no hammah
In dis lan',
Strikes lak mine, bebby,
Strikes lak mine

He sang loud enough to be heard through the breathing mask. The sound surprised everyone. The older man woke up. He even chuckled to himself. He tried to imagine why anyone would sing about pounding a nail, something he recalled from his youth seeing his grandfather do, or maybe it had been an uncle.

The old man's lightened mood calmed the Prisoner even as the song dredged up the ever present anger that he struggled with in order to keep production levels high. He knew full well what the song was about. He had talked to old prisoners who had been part of an experiment, a return to breaking rocks, actually recycling cement. The guards had been so entertained by the novelty that they'd bet on which inmate would pass out first in the process of hammering virtually nonstop. There had been all sorts of injuries, with the men blind from sweat and disoriented from exhaustion.

The Prisoner decided to let everyone off early, or perhaps the singing made the time go by quickly. Who could know?

Nat was still singing when the cell went transparent. As the stations were folded, the other men became aware of the man Nat replaced. The man was trembling, but not as he had been when gripped by the sickness. His eyes were open. Flecks of white spit jumped from his lips as he struggled to speak.

"That's, that's that crying, hoodoo music," he finally managed. "You trying to kill somebody!"

With that, the man scrambled to his feet. Lying on the floor, he had seemed a good size, but standing, he appeared huge. Everyone was so surprised to see him rise that they were unprepared for his amazingly quick lunge at Nat. His hands were like a sandpaper vice around Nat's neck. The air rushed from Nat's throat in a second. The other men were awake but tired and, even working together, could not pry the man's hands from Nat's neck. The Prisoner summoned guards, but Nat had passed out by the time they arrived.

Nat awoke in what he would later learn was the detention facility, the prison within the prison, the place where altercations or rebellions would land you. With its opaque walls, it was more like a regular room than the cells. In the cells, you had to look down through the layers and layers of glass to see anything as opaque as the walls in this room.

Besides the opaqueness, the humidity was noticeably higher in this place than it had been in the cell. The floor and lower parts of the wall were moist to the touch. The ceiling dripped in places. He heard thunder and what had to be rain just before he fell back into unconsciousness.

When Nat awoke again, it was to the sputtering and sparks of a huge flat screen that had been jerry-rigged into the moist, dripping ceiling. The puddles on the floor distracted him from the sparks until coughing erupted from the screen, and then a voice.

"Just wanted you to know—"

There was a jagged flash of electricity between the screen and the raggedy hole that been cut to put the screen into the ceiling. Nat tried to rouse himself to find a dry place on the floor.

The voice in the screen was speaking, but not to him.

"... and if he dies in there, it won't do us any good whatsoever. What's the difference?"

With those words, the screen and the entire room went black. It became harder to find dry spots on the floor. Water seeped into his shoes, no matter where he stood. The thunder was close enough to rattle what he'd thought were very solid walls and shake more water from the ceiling. Short bursts of noise leapt from his throat out of his control as he sloshed from one corner to another. He walked along every inch of wall and floor to somehow find a place where the water was not rising. There was no such place, and when the water reached his thighs, even the noises in his throat died.

Soon, the water was high enough for him to float and then just high enough for him to touch the ceiling. He could try to pry the screen from the ceiling to see if the hole into which it had been so sloppily placed actually led anywhere. Even the fear of possibly electrocuting himself meant nothing in the face of certain drowning. He had to feel in the dark and quickly. He wished he'd had the presence of mind to get naked before the water had gotten so high. His heavy, wet shoes and clothing felt like animals working to drag him under. His arms quickly became tired as he paddled to stay afloat when he wasn't flailing about, feeling for the screen in the ceiling. Water slopped into his eyes, nose, and mouth.

Feeling around the ceiling, he grabbed something hot to the touch, the prong-shaped object. He couldn't hold on. His limbs stiffened. There was water in his ears, eyes, nose, and mouth. He was gulping water and it was becoming harder to reach for the ceiling. He realized it was because the water was suddenly receding. He choked on a mouthful of water and hoped his strength would last until his feet could touch the floor. As he began to fade there were voices, snatches of words.

"Slower"

"No . . . Warden . . . death . . . scandal."

***

He was happy that the room they placed him in was overheated since they'd taken his wet clothes and given him a thin blanket to wrap himself in. A guard dressed in a uniform Nat hadn't seen before brought him dry clothes.

In what he assumed was the Warden's office, he suddenly felt the urge to stand even though his legs shook with nerves and weakness. He'd had no sense of time in the black room where he nearly drowned and had come close to electrocution. How long had he been paddling, treading water, reaching for the screen? There was some soreness in his right shoulder from grasping to try to pry it loose, and numbness in his hand that might have come from the blood draining out of it as he had been holding it up, or was it from the electrical shock?

There was rumbling outside, above. He didn't want to think about thunder.

The person he presumed was the Warden walked in flanked by two armored guards. Nat had heard about guards modi-fied with armor. They even showered inside the shells that had become extensions of their virtually impenetrable skin. He decided to sit down. The three men continued to walk to the Warden's desk area. Their steps sounded sharp but did not echo. The room had been conditioned, no surprise there.

The Warden went behind his desk and produced, with a touch, the smallest, sleekest printer Nat had ever seen. It was perhaps four feet wide and no more than a foot tall, clearly specialized, very quiet. But there was a smell. In a moment, it produced the most magnificent, seemingly wooden guitar Nat had ever seen. It was all he could do not to reach for it.

The Warden smiled at Nat's obvious desire. Nat stood, staring at the guitar, as one of the guards walked it over to him. It was cold to the touch, smooth, almost to the point of being soft and perfectly tuned.

***

The rooms where Nat played for the Warden and his guests were strangely conditioned. Sometimes, they were quiet and comfortable. Sometimes, there were voices of people who were not present. Sometimes, all the other people in the room were white. Sometimes the Warden was one of maybe two white people in the room.

When Nat wasn't performing, he slept in a part of the prison he'd never so much as knew existed. He had his own room. But he spent most of the time in the common area trying to talk to people, though he got the feeling talking was discouraged.

The rooms were regular rooms with opaque walls. But the light in them seemed like sunlight and it was impossible to tell from which direction it came. The tables and chairs were a mishmash of materials and styles. The inmates had developed gangs and cliques. Nat was one of the few who had no clique. He felt vulnerable, naked.

He tried to talk to a man with a very strange looking stringed instrument. The man had grooves in his cheeks that had been intentionally placed there. His instrument was a big round gourd that had been sliced in half so it had a flat surface. There was one big pole sticking out of it with taut strings and two smaller poles. The man would sit the big gourd on the ground between his legs, place his fingers on the two small poles, and pluck the strings with his thumbs. It produced the most melodic and harp-like sound.

The man was friendly enough, but did not speak English. Nat didn't even know what language the man spoke. Nonetheless, it was clear that he wanted to be friends. So he and Nat found a corner and began to try to play together, which was much easier than talking. Nat learned the instrument was called a kora. When Nat asked the Warden if he and the man with the kora could play together for one of the audiences, the Warden simply smiled slowly without opening his mouth. Nat never saw the man with the kora again.

After a few days, Nat was plagued with nightmares about the kora player in the water room with the screen in the ceiling shooting bolts. The water rose and did not recede.

Nat took on more and more of what he discerned were night performances. He had little sense of day or night. But he realized the nightmares were fewer if he just took catnaps in the common area.

The Warden had Nat playing more and more often. The audiences varied in size but they always wore extraordinarily refined clothing. He was usually close enough to see diamonds or gold in their discrete piercings, close enough to see what could only be the finest animal furs woven into their garments, close enough to hear conversations before the show about exclusive travel arrangements or live performances featuring people that the masses could only see via hologram if they were lucky.

Try as they might, no matter how grand the room, the technicians assigned to it could not completely block the rumble of thunder. So the topic of conversations that most intrigued and worried Nat was the one he heard the least. He gathered there was a huge storm either coming to the area, or already there, or perhaps a nearly continuous series of storms. He didn't need to overhear conversations to know who would be dying by the boatload as a result of the storms. All he could do was worry and hope for the people he knew.

While some members of his audience were more knowledgeable about the music than Nat, many seemed content with the prestige of the event. They were the ones who simply wanted him to play louder and faster to distract them from the rumble. One even brought in a freestanding unit to amplify Nat and the guitar. That person was removed when the Warden discovered it.

One fateful performance, there were some very somber looking women in the front row. They all had very fine dark clothing. The only thing that announced they were in uniform was that they each had identical ear units with barely visible links to the eyes running just below their eyebrows. There were three of them, and the Leader could have been the daughter or perhaps granddaughter of the dark-skinned woman from the emporium, Nat's teacher.

The Warden attended to these women and the Leader in particular. This was the only time Nat had heard him ask permission to sit next to anyone. The Leader's smile showed clear indifference to the Warden's request. During the show, she surprised Nat with a request for a song by Memphis Minnie.

I works on the levee mama both night and day
I works on the levee mama both night and day
I ain't got nobody, keep the water away
Oh cryin' won't help you, prayin' won't do no good
Oh cryin' won't help you, prayin' won't do no good
When the levee breaks, mama, you got to lose

Nat was impressed that such a young woman knew such an old song. He smiled at her. She smiled back and grasped the hand of the woman next to her.

"She was singing that song when I met her," the Leader said after the performance.

Nat couldn't imagine where anyone would have been playing Memphis Minnie in public and so imagined a private setting. But why "When the Levee Breaks?" It was not the most romantic song he could imagine playing. In fact, he tried not to channel Memphis Minnie's plaintive, hopeless resolve because it affected him so. The song of the rising water made him think of the end of the world even before he'd almost died in the room with the ceiling screen.

By the end of the show, the rumbling was too loud for Nat to be heard. The Leader and the Warden were in a corner of the room having an intense discussion. One of the few things Nat grasped from the conversation was the leader saying, "It's that or the war."

The next morning, Nat found himself in a rescue simulation trainer after being told he would have a great opportunity to reduce his prison time. The news of his being assigned to a rescue flight somehow made it down to the general population. There were others assigned to the mission as well. The inmates who had not been assigned to rescue mostly avoided the handful that had. Others shook their heads, smirked, and chuckled derisively at the "chosen few."

The two hours in rescue simulation were jarring enough. At one point Nat came close to throwing up, as he was certain that the severed limb on the "floor" was real. But those two rough hours weren't nearly enough to prepare him or anyone for the actual flight.

The open sky with storm would have been a fearful sight from the ground. But to be thrust directly into it after many days of incarceration was bloodcurdling. The co-pilot "trainer" wasn't much help, as he was almost as frightened as Nat and thus barely communicative.

It was hard to believe the storm was "on it's last leg" as the co-pilot said. The rain was relentless, horizontal. The wiper shields kept the windows clear, but that almost made things worse, as they had a very clear view of just how bad things were. Nat was certain two gray-black masses of swirling air to the east and west were tornadoes. They were filled with what could have been people or debris. The copilot broke his near silence to tell some convoluted lie about the funnels not being tornadoes. Fortunately, both of the deadly swirling masses were moving away from them.

"Don't be looking in the distance," the copilot admonished. "There's gonna be people right below us. That's why we're here."

With that, the copilot began tagging buildings with his scanner, marking structures with the numbers of living and dead where either were close enough to the exterior to be found, and zapping the odd stray animal in the process.

When it came time for Nat to take the controls, he was fitted with a round band that bit into his head. He couldn't tell what it was made of, only that it sent waves of pain through his skull. He could barely keep the machine aloft even with the copilot "helping," in part because Nat now had access to the copilot's mental state and the amazing fear the other man tried to fight off. Controlling the craft also took a backseat to thinking about the pain from the primitive probe.

Nat's direct mental commands did nothing to control the flying machine. But playing music in his head helped him level it off. It also helped when he tried to imagine what the Leader and the Warden had been talking about at the concert. That is what he was thinking about when the copilot disappeared, vanishing in thin air. Had the trainer not been there to begin with? If not, why had he been so frightened?

After flying alone, marking buildings, and even transporting the odd surface survivor, Nat heard the Singer.

***

The Scientist was desperate to hold his job. His wife the Author's work hadn't taken off quite yet. The Girl had yet to edit the story down to something simple, something that did not both eat and birth itself simultaneously, fascinating as the Girl thought that was.

"If you can't make or sell widgets, you have to sell the story of widgets, not the real story with the missing and overlapping pieces, but the straight story, the story story."

"The missing and overlapping parts *are* the story story."

"Mom, please, you know what I mean!"

The Scientist caught only bits of their back and forth and was prone to ponder them for much longer than he thought was productive. But it was a way of connecting, in a manner of speaking, to the rest of his family, reminding himself why he was completely alone.

What made the Scientist rise obscenely early in the morning was the desire to somehow craft a way to tell people what it was he did. It would have to be some combination of hologram, speaking, and writing, or maybe music. If he could find music that was slow and serious but could still lay in the background like a dark wall, music that drew just enough attention to itself, but not too much, that was the goal. Or maybe just a simple hologram of him singing the explanation of what he did would work. Or maybe he could learn to work one of those dead, android-like things and pretend it was talking instead of him, and have them both in a hologram. He was scanning his implant, thinking he would pursue all of the above, when something snagged his attention. The singing he was listening to lagged over from an almost skipped image. It captivated him so. He put it into the room there with him. He knew the sound was opera, that it was another language, Italian. But what he knew for sure, though the language was beyond him, was that the singer was pleading.

> Vissi d'arte, vissi d'amore,
> non feci mai male ad anima viva!

He was soon inconsolable over words he could not translate.

> Nell'ora del dolor
> perchè, perchè, Signor,
> ah, perchè me ne rimuneri così?

In the spotlight of what seemed like a small room was the singer with a veil, dressed in white, with red gloves and red cloth shoes and a red waistcloth. Standing on her lap was a dead android figure with leaves over its breasts and vagina. It was supposed to be singing. The real singer's face barely moved. Occasionally, she would look to the edges of the light where other people's clothing and silhouettes were just visible.

***

The Scientist was almost afraid to find the translation of the song, lest it prove to be not as moving as the sound or, though it seemed impossible, more moving than the raw sound of the music. But he did learn that the figure whose lips moved as the singer sang was called a "dummy." Even after learning that, he couldn't help but think of the word "surrogate," though he knew it was dead, virtually hollow, as he determined that the singer had her arm inside the figure.

She would have a hard time recalling where she had last heard the song. Then, later, on the way to prison to visit her father, it would come back to her, in waves.

*****

Initially, the Scientist thought the dummy would be a good filter through which he could finally speak without inducing sleep, though he was also concerned. All of the surrogates seemed so strange and comical. How or where in the world could he possibly find a figure that would not make people laugh?

No one laughed when he spoke, and thus, the perfect dummy would be one that looked quite like him. He could print one from a combination of his photo for the face and, for the body, images of other surrogates.

As was noted in the early twenty-first century, before advanced printing, there is a space in human mimicry that leaves humans unsettled. The early devices produced mimics that were ghastly, not quite complete, not quite copies, not quite human. Children in particular felt a great discomfort seeing these creations that fell into the eerie zone between human and non-human faces. These days, it is difficult to reproduce those sorts of undead, nightmarish features because the printers reject them or jam up and have to be cleared.

But the Scientist, almost like an adolescent male prankster, overrode the printer because he was so desperate to get it right. Ironically, he got the same frightening results as the pranksters, dummies with freakishly disquieting facial oddities. In this case, the dummies had subtle but horrible creases around the eyes that made them seem less like facial features and more like creatures in their own right. Try as he might, he could not stop himself from stopping the machine before it had finished printing and so all the results were horrifying. His obsession with interrupting the printer's cycle was powered by something at the bottom of his thinking, something kept just out of reach by frustration, something welded to the experience of fixing the interview machine that had malfunctioned during the Author's interview, the great and fortuitous accident that had brought them together.

He succeeded with one goal, to be sure. He knew no one was going to laugh at the dummy that was supposed to speak in his stead. Even he, its creator, was barely able to focus on its face without turning away. Nonetheless, he was not ready to abandon the idea of speaking through the surrogate, teaching himself to speak without moving his lips.

He spent hours unearthing a serviceable singing voice. He taught himself the phonetics of the language sung by the Veiled Woman and her surrogate and fought the inclination to translate the song. This, he told himself, was in preparation for one last presentation to the CEO of his company to get his job back. In truth, he was in the thrall of the Veiled Woman, not so much in love with her as addicted to seeing and hearing her.

He woke up looking forward to sitting in front of the primitive external screen and listening to the voice that only it could emit. He wondered about the people who had been so insightful as to provide her a place, a platform to ply her extraordinary craft. He envied those in the audience. He pictured himself as one of them, people at the edge of her light.

***

One early morning, before the Bird arrived at her window, the Girl lay awake contemplating the logistical and economic challenges of running away to be with Nat and Tina. She heard the aria "Vissi d'Arte" drifting through the house. She knew the song from one of her opera freak friends whom the Bird also visited. Her friend had translated the aria, and the Girl, thinking of the translation, assumed it was her mother, the Author, playing the music.

Days and days later, one of the last things she would do for the Scientist before leaving the house would be to give him the translation. He read it and put his head in his hands. Water seeped between his fingers. She regretted what she had thought of him all these years and put her arms around him. She even suppressed the urge to draw back in horror when she glimpsed the small pile of figures that were not quite him laying crumpled in the corner of the room with their ghastly eyes.

***

A day or so later, the Scientist was riding along holding his surrogate in an opaque plastic bag on the seat next to him. He'd made a physical appointment to get in line for a lottery ticket that might allow him to speak with the CEO of his company. Part of the transport was in total darkness so as to obscure the route.

When he finally reached the ticket line, he found people in a joyous mood as if waiting for an amusement gram. It lifted his own spirits to the point where he felt like chatting with the others in line, many of whom wanted to know what was in the plastic bag.

Eventually, security beamed in to find out why so many people had laid down in line. By that time, the Scientist had moved many places ahead of what was becoming a pile of sleepers.

He was less than ten places from a lottery ticket when security pounced. They grabbed him and those ahead of him in line who were still awake and began an interrogation.

The Scientist had never been more frightened. He spoke rapidly, and loudly, desperate to get back to the line. The others who had been in line with him were the first to fade, their knees buckling and heads nodding despite their wanting to remain upright and alert in the presence of such fearsome security units. But the security units themselves began to succumb, to feel woozy and heavy headed.

The utter fear the Scientist felt at that moment reminded him of the fear that had led him to seek out the CEO in the first place. He needed to help his family. He felt his daughter slipping away and his wife being stuck into some unshapely hole of a career, and they would still have no good means of surviving, and he would be isolated at home with no colleagues, no work. So he began to edge slowly backward toward one of the ticket dispenser areas.

It wasn't until he got home and was showing the lottery ticket to his family that it dawned on him he'd left the plastic bag with the surrogate behind. It came to him as he watched them watching a news gram about a "dead android" with eyes that appeared to want to crawl off of its face. Officials in the penal system thought the thing was a brilliant creation and were scrambling to find some uses for it and to find its creator, pretending, for some reason, that they hadn't already scanned the object for its maker's identity.

At that point, the news gram was interrupted by the CEO's security detail appearing in the family's house. Not grams but the real things, their muscles bulging through their orange lizard scale armor. Only one had a weapon. He'd also been modified with a spiked tail. They put the Scientist on an exclusive transport bound for the top office.

***

Though the people making the orders had no clear idea of what they would do with the units, orders for the dead android were pouring in from his friends who ran penal facilities, and the CEO wanted to be in on fulfilling the orders. The dead android was going be a goldmine, another platinum news gram for the collection. It was exciting because it was so crude and unexpected. The media in people's implants all but throbbed as it consumed and resold the info.

Given all of this, the temptation was overwhelming for the CEO to listen in on his under partners' conversations with the creator. Unbeknownst to even them, the CEO planned to summarily dump the Scientist after they'd made a good gram of him and he had revealed exactly where and how he'd stopped the printer to get the eyes just right. The CEO planned to give the Scientist a good chunk of money. But any demands for his fair share of the stream would fall on deaf ears.

What pushed the CEO to listen, albeit via external screen, and what distracted him from listening was the usual when he became overly excited—an earworm attack. He was, in fact, still a bit woozy from sleep aids and anti-hallucinogens taken the night before. But the sloshing sound and the familiar whisper of the voice that had no place, "What's really in there?" and the mantralike repetition were all too recognizable and rising like foul water.

Deciding whether or not to listen in on the interrogation was as close as he ever came to questioning himself. He left the images flat on the screen but closed the audio, at least at first.

The CEO's screen revealed what he'd gathered and feared, group after group of macho interrogators became drowsy, unwilling to admit that they could not listen to the Scientist without falling out. Finally, one woman interrogator fitted herself with a probe and began the interrogation via screen only. For a while there was silence as their exchanges appeared in front of them. The CEO opened the screen into a gram and with it came the audio, which was now only the room ambiance.

The woman was fascinated with the Scientist's work on sharing consciousness without probes. He seemed on the verge of a monumental breakthrough if only he could get someone besides his wife and daughter to listen. With the mention of his wife and daughter, the aria from Tosca blossomed in his head. Some of the words made it to the screen in English and others in Italian. None of the music translated. The program seized up and men watching from behind glass all but pushed the woman aside and restarted the verbal interrogation.

Now, the temptation for the CEO to hear the infamous voice of the Scientist was too great. Just a snippet he thought, surely I could survive that. It took but a moment or two for the interrogators in the room to pass out, and the CEO fell asleep shortly thereafter.

When he awoke, he thought he was still dreaming. There was no trace of the earworm. He was almost frightened. He tried purposefully to recall the Bird's sound. He brought it up and dismissed it with ease. He almost drafted parchment then and there that would grant the Scientist a fare share of the two streams, one for the dead surrogate and one for the earworm cure. Instead he closed all lines and became inexplicably absent.

When he returned, satiated from days of debauchery, he engaged the Scientist with a probe and cut a deal. The CEO would provide the Scientist access to his friends with the earworm, and he and the Scientist would split what the Scientist thought was an enormous fee. The Scientist agreed to it instantly. The walls of the room seemed to open as he all but leapt from his seat after his bios scanned through the parchment. He would return home triumphant. His family would not lose their home. His wife would not have to write those dreadful stories fit only for entertainment grams. His daughter would receive elite training.

What he didn't know was that his daughter had left home after the second week of his absence. Security had prevented even the most basic communication with his family. Concern over the fate of the Scientist had left her and her mother distraught. The Author had tried to bury herself in her work. The Girl had taken to feeding the Bird more and more so that it would come more often. It became even chubbier and its song more robust. The Girl debated with herself. Was her hearing improving? Regardless, she loved the sound of the Bird. Her mother, on the other hand, did not. They tried not to argue. But it was no use. The link between the Bird and the Singer was unknown to the Author but was a beacon to the Girl, and, when things at home came to the breaking point, the Girl boarded a transport and sought out Nat and Tina.

The Scientist did not communicate with his family until he got home. Most of the joy he'd felt about his new position was lost with the Girl gone. The Author never thought she'd long to hear the disgusting, misshapen Bird. But she longed for any sign of the Girl.

***

It is hard to see your home until you leave it. The further the Girl got from home the clearer it became, especially in the moments that felt like gaps, spaces between intentions. It was there she found all the things she could have said and, just as importantly, recalled the true weight of idle moments. The Bird flew in the window and sat before it sang. Her mother had finished writing and stared out of the window. Her father closed his eyes with his ever placid face over a small hand screen of formulas. The three of them sat in a moment where no one spoke at the dinner table. One of them smiled a blank, reflexive smile and the others smiled back just as reflexively, and suddenly, because they came all at once, the smiles were not so blank.

Then there was the Bird. It refused to follow her. Assuming someone remembered to feed it, she would have to return home to see it.

The trip felt longer than it actually took and she fell asleep on the transport. Normally, this would not have been a problem, but the operators who were supposed to rouse sleepers before the end of the line were distracted by a gram, a rumor really, that a cure for the earworm had been discovered. They were all fascinated even after they admitted they didn't know anyone with the worm.

The Girl wound up at the end of the transport line in the dark with barely enough money to get back to her destination. Even so, the transports wouldn't cycle back up for hours. She was hungry and panicked. The operators that were supposed to have sent signals through the car to rouse her were now walking through the unit kicking people off, and they weren't too kind about it. She jumped from her seat and began to grab her belongings to avoid being slammed around like some of the sleeping and disheveled folks in other parts of the car.

She noticed that one person of indeterminate gender and dressed rather well to be on a transport did not seem concerned about being tossed about, was not excited, but moving deliberately as if it were normal to be getting off here where everyone else was kicked off. The calmness the Girl saw on the person's face turned to sadness when their eyes met. The person looked at the Girl's mismatched possessions and tried to smile bravely as if to encourage her, but the smile took a bit too much effort.

The Girl noticed the operators were closing in and she continued to gather her things to exit the transport. The Person followed her.

"Do you have a place?"

It was one thing to exchange half smiles with a stranger on the transport. Conversation was another level of engagement. The Girl wanted to act as though she hadn't heard the person speak. But, off the transport, in the hustle of the overly bright city, she relented.

"Not here," she replied, unable to hide her uneasiness.

"That's fairly obvious. I've never seen you in the car."

"You always take it to the end and in those clothes?"

"You wear what you have. There is a place I can show you. It's not much to speak of, but it's safe."

The Girl decided to follow the person. Their destination was a few units away. Fewer and fewer people were on the street, but it became noticeably louder. Their clothing was dull. Most of the people were dark. Hair mods abounded, especially with the women and the neutral gendered.

"I'm Gen," said the person. "Do you prefer a name?"

Gen, boy that's original, thought the Girl. *Why not just call yourself person?* But she kept those thoughts to herself. The Person, Gen, was showing her kindness.

When Gen and the Girl entered the place where Gen lived, the silence was the first thing the Girl noticed, perhaps because it had been so loud outside. What's more, it was a large open area crowded with young people with trendy, homemade mods; fake third eyes; heart-shaped lips and foreheads and cheeks with the glowing red circled A. Most wore probes of some type. There were many doors on one side and in the wall facing the door. She assumed they opened to sleeping units.

How and why did so many people—there must have been fifty or so—stay so quiet? It seemed unlikely they had the money to condition the place. But who knew?

"They let her sleep past her stop," Gen announced to the group, "and she has no preference."

***

Tina was on stage giving it all she had, as usual. It was only when she stopped singing that she noticed sweat was stinging her eyes. She wiped them for relief and in the hopes that she was not seeing what she thought she saw. The level of noise in the place dropped when she went silent. She could almost hear the noise of the scuffle she saw off to her right where other audience members were clearing away. Two people were trying to subdue a third person who had steel blue skin.

Where was security? In a moment there would be chaos. Nat jumped from the stage with his guitar. The crowd noise was up again. Those who hadn't yet noticed the fight closed in around Nat, thinking he'd come to be with them. They stepped back when he swung the instrument off his shoulder and held the neck with both hands like a bat.

The steel blue creature turned just in time to take the blow from the instrument full in the face. It staggered but seemed like it would recover. Nat struck again and it fell.

***

There had been violence now at three shows in a row. Horrific wounds were sold to low-end screeners. Nat and Tina and other Revue members had nightmares full of screaming, bloodied fans. Still, the dismissive bluster of some in the Revue who had returned to society was now replaced with an even more cynical resolve.

Nat was the exception. Even the ugliness of prison had not hardened him to where he could rest with pleas for mercy from innocent fans. It spun in his head day and night. It distracted him during rehearsal. He'd almost swallowed a mod offered by one of the singers. He'd confronted her earlier because he thought she was an addict. He only refused the offer when he noticed the sexual glint in the woman's expression and realized he would be accepting more than the drug.

He had become more rigidly monogamous and regimented as the tour had become more successful. He was always practicing or recording. The constant and detailed scheduling felt somehow like the opposite of prison, even as something about having been in prison drove him to nail down as much time as possible. The free moments he had, he spent with Tina. It was the only time he was not focused on a current or future task. Even so, when he was not with her, he kept planning to ask her not to dance so provocatively on stage. It seemed wrong in public, somehow.

After a minor surge because of the publicity, show attendance dropped because of the violence. The sparser crowds included more people with head and neck mods. Nat thought he recognized a few people from LJ's.

The Revue's meetings had become subdued. Tina didn't have to make the usual repeated calls to order. No one was discussing the crowd reaction to a particular song or new improvised section. The direct security were particularly low key, having been probed into depression. Someone or something at the shows was digging deep enough into the security folks to make them all but immobile when the attacks were happening. A few had quit. No one had so much as applied to be added to the force, even with increased pay.

The Security that had stayed on were always looking to prove themselves. This only heightened tension in the Revue. They scared people during one meeting when the alarms sounded. One even forgot the rule about weapons at meetings and nearly brandished hers when the alarm voice noted two figures the system had never scanned approaching the east door. She put her weapon away when the Girl and a quite forlorn Gen came to the screen. They hugged for what seemed like forever. After that, the Girl looked sad. Everyone watching felt they were watching a final farewell.

***

The Girl was torn. On the one hand, she had set out to join Nat and Tina's Revue and she'd finally made it to the door. The people in the house with Gen had not been easy to live with. Still, the place fascinated her.

It was there she had learned how sound was encrypted at the weapons factory to pass sensitive data from one monitored printer to the next to create the most sophisticated weapons, hot borders, and robot defense grids. Very few outside of the house or the plant Gen infiltrated suspected anything as primitive as sound could, or would, be used to create such complex real and virtual weapons.

Gen was one of the rare workers whose brain could encrypt. House members would painstakingly download seemingly innocuous scraps left in Gen's implants and decode the information. The Girl had immersed herself in the coding and unraveling of the barriers between nations such that she felt she could travel anywhere in the world without a visa, though, for some reason, she had little desire to try.

But the most significant thing the Girl had learned at the house with Gen, the thing she was most anxious to share with the Revue, was how to tell stories. All the formulas for coding and decryption were memorized and passed on orally with fetishistic attention to detail. The training for this began with learning and reciting old stories. Rooms in the house were filled with handbooks, some of which were hundreds of years old, fragile, brittle, and hardly ever brought out into the light. The frail condition of the books further inspired people in the house to memorize the stories. It had become one more thing—not to commit to writing—along with the house security measures. As much as she loved holding the contours of stories in her mind, the Girl had mixed feelings about the high place oral storytelling held in the culture of the house, which included passing stories orally.

"The stories are great, but I don't hear that well," the Girl said defiantly at one house meeting. "What am I supposed to do? You gonna pay for my modification? No! I read stories, that's how I memorize."

No one spoke at first. The young man facilitating the meeting looked sheepish but tried to sound firm and confident.

"Reading isn't stories. It's just words."

***

Everyone in the Revue was suspicious of the Girl for some time. Nat paid perhaps the least attention to her and Tina was the first to warm up to her.

"I've never been one for security clearances," she'd said to the Girl after a rehearsal. "They'll always find what they're looking for, even if it's not there. Might as well be open."

The Girl smiled broadly, could not control herself, and rushed to embrace a surprised Tina. She responded to the Girl's embrace knowing only that they both needed to be held at that moment.

After that, the Girl felt she had nothing to hide and began to tell Tina what she'd learned at the House, how modern weapons and company security were coded in rudimentary sounds she had learned to unravel. Tina was troubled by what she heard. The Girl was on the verge of being a woman, but, Tina felt, was still too young for what she was carrying around. Nonetheless, she thought the Girl should present to the group in the hopes of decommissioning the units that were disrupting the shows.

"There is the sound and the thing that produces the sound. We think about them together, but as we know they're separate things: the bell is not the ringing. Well, some folks have learned to blend certain electrical impulses, really to copy what goes on when we imagine a sound in our heads and turn that into a weapon. Who would have thought such a sliver of a thing could ever leave our heads let alone become a force?"

Nat was interested but distracted. Other Revue members became restless and rude during the Girl's presentation. Violence at the shows was their main focus and preoccupation. Few, if any, were interested in how corporations had come to blend sounds and their sources until the Girl made a connection.

"If you give me one of the fallen units from the attacks at the concert, I can trace it. Of course, once we find the company sponsor, what are we going to do about it? I mean, I guess it's good information even if we can't really, you know, do anything with it."

She now had the full attention of everyone in the room, most especially Nat's. The idea of tracing the units made his pulse quicken. But then reality chimed in. The Girl was right. Even if they found out which corporation was sending the attackers, what could they do about?

Nat recalled the period when he truly began to understand slavery, how it shaped the world he shared with the non-dark people. The history he lived with. The barbaric attacks on innocent fans felt like something else.

The Girl had put plain light on what had been there for all to see, the problem with the companies, the wealth compounded with control, how even such a minor disruption and breaking of certain rules couldn't be tolerated by certain people with power. That was his analysis. He didn't know how the Bird and its earworm sound were connected to people being slashed, hacked, and knocked unconscious.

What had his mentor, the Old Woman, lived through? Things hinted at from the times she had lashed out at him? Where was the teacher who played the trumpet in school? What had happened to the inmates that could not sing and play, to the man with the kora? The only people he'd ever seen that were close to being free and happy were the ones running the prison, and some of them would have been happy to let him drown during the storm. None of it was enough. Now, they were opening the skulls of people who had come to see him do the one thing that drew him close to any semblance of happiness. His anger was so sudden and fearful that, for a moment, he was paralyzed. The grim stupor gripped him and passed, but the rawness that fueled it imploded and compacted.

***

Members of the Revue were more than happy to take time off from touring to let the Girl explain how to trace units to their companies of origin, to sort through the layers of subsidiaries and get to the principal. There were mixed opinions on what to do, though.

"Why don't we shame and expose the subsidiaries too? They're just as bad as the root corporation," said the drummer.

"I say we take a break from the stage and chill for a while, wait this thing out," said the pianist.

"Take a break, yes, but only to search out these sons-of-bitches. I want to feel somebody's throat in my fists," said the trumpet player.

Tina, exasperated, rose and spoke, at first a bit too loudly, and everyone had to slam their hands over their ears to prevent damage. She modulated her volume.

"We don't even know who these people are or why the hell we're their targets," she said as she sat back down. "At least let her finish telling us what the deal is," she said, turning to the wiry, dark trumpet player, "before you start crushing people's windpipes."

Nat slipped out of the meeting. He was ashamed of feeling like the trumpeter, having the urge to feel the life being forced from someone's body in retribution for the concert violence and all the things that had become tangled with it in his mind. He would never be able to admit that to Tina. But he had found a glimmer of hope, if not redemption, when something the Girl said clicked with his memory of the rescue mission. He went to his room to find the old probe.

***

The Scientist and the Author were using copious amounts of their now substantial combined revenue streams to search for their daughter. The firms they employed were among the best. At least one had been used by the first CEO who had used the sleeping cure. None of them had any experience with the more primitive methods of trail encryption the Girl had learned from Gen and company.

Months passed. The only thing that lifted the parents' spirits was the occasional lurid pink feather they would find in the Girl's room or loads of crap the bird left outside of the window. They never saw or heard the creature itself. The Author had dreams where she and the Scientist would "discover" that the feathers and the droppings were hallucinations, mirages they had deluded themselves into seeing. She would awake just as they fell despairingly into each other's arms.

One day, the Scientist arrived at the home of one of his wealthy repeat customers only to find the place surrounded by security. He'd seen lights from a distance but had assumed it couldn't have been his client's location where the incident was taking place, since the Scientist had received no call or signal of any type.

When he got close enough for the elite frequency sirens to be picked up by anyone, security confronted his transport unit and insisted he come inside. They refused to answer his questions but bombarded him with their own. It wasn't until they allowed him to re-board his transport and head home that he discovered the woman whose condition he'd come to check on was dead.

She was the first of his clients to die. When the third one died, the Scientist relented to the Author's advice to seek legal counsel. By the fourth death, he was in custody. When a fifth death occurred, the outcry from corporate sectors for his punishment was so great that authorities scheduled his trial. This, despite the fact that the fifth murder took place while he was in custody.

It seemed nothing could save him. The prosecution argued that the Scientist could have timed the murder to occur while he was detained, to throw them off. The fact that he would lose serious revenue once his clients died meant nothing next to the utter befuddlement of the authorities. The closest thing they had to a clue was that the Scientist was the only thing all the victims had in common. Attempts by the less elite wealthy clients to save him were utterly thwarted by stories bought and sold by the most elite clients who had been completely cured, in no small part because they were late to the party and still needed treatment. Stories of vengeance sold well on all platforms, and the wealthy needed vengeance.

The Scientist could only reflect on all of this since they'd done outpatient mod to prevent him from speaking lest the guards and who knows who else might fall prey to his sleep-inducing verbiage.

***

Murder had not been a conscious, preplanned goal when Nat first learned to trace units to sources and then sources to principal shareholders. Even after he screened the story of his mentor, the Old Woman being picked up on some fanciful charge because she'd been linked to him, he had no conscious plans to take anyone's life.

Indeed, he wasn't even sure that the probe, even with the mods the Girl suggested, would allow him to drift under the security of the locations he visited. He was amazed and heartened to discover that the old-style probe and sound synthesis completely undid the security systems and live security units, disabled the former and paralyzed the latter. He walked in on the wealthiest of the wealthy unannounced, often waiting for them to get dressed and enter the receiving area, as they always assumed only welcome guests could make it into their inner sanctums.

He began by introducing himself, though some knew who he was. He produced pictures of concertgoers who had been victimized by the "security" units sent by the companies to which the rich person belonged. If his host had posted writings about live shows and earworms, Nat showed their news screens. He then laid out the case that made it clear that the earworm was caused by the Bird and the Bird alone, and that live performance had nothing to do with the affliction. Ideally, he wanted to get to the part about how the ever-warming planet was what enticed the bird to move so far north in the first place. In any event, there was, he stressed, no connection between the earworm and any live performances, including those by the Nat and Tina Turner Revue.

Reactions to his presence and presentation ranged from laughter to horror, from serious engagement to utter silence. Eventually, the security units would begin to wake and were able to move. The first time this happened, Nat panicked and lurched through the probe to re-engage and subdue the security units again.

The sudden movement back into the units permanently damaged or injured several of them, but no one realized this until much later. His panicky reaction also stunned the people Nat had come to speak with. He pulled back, shocked, when he realized the probes he'd used to break security had put him in their minds. He tried to pull away. But he found that he was also pulling out of the security units and that would be his undoing. So he re-engaged to knock out the units. As a result, sometimes the person he'd come to speak with appeared to fall asleep. If not, he would probe them for the root of the thought that live shows were connected to earworms. Could he undo the connections? It was tempting. But he didn't have the skill, and when those who had managed to stay awake when he had first entered them fell like ragdolls, he would leave. There was no trace of his visit.

***

The Scientist, who had spent a great deal of his time avoiding interaction or desperately trying to figure out how to make it work, now found himself with more different kinds of people than ever before. Some inmates felt sorry for him when they learned he had been modified and that he couldn't speak. Some found it frustrating and used the influence they had (he was in a relatively high-end unit) to move him or be moved themselves. Soon he wound up with one cellmate who talked incessantly. He learned more about the man than he knew of his own daughter. Thoughts of his wife and daughter were his shield against the onslaught of words.

The Author's visits were the only time he was released from modification. But those meetings were timed and brief. During one such visit, his wife entered looking happy but very tired. She did not let him speak and came in only long enough to tell him that he should steel himself. When he appeared ready, she left, and the Girl entered the room.

When she had set out to visit her father, The Girl had been anxious and in a hurry. But she had to move slowly and deliberately so as not to be trailed from Nat and Tina's. It took more than a day for all of the tracking devices to fall neutral. It took all of her will not to respond with excitement. While she had had sporadic contact with her mother, she had not seen her father for what seemed like a very long time. But even the inner joy she held to herself was short-lived and was replaced with a mix of relief and despair when she actually saw him.

There was an initial spark to his face when he first saw her. They could not touch, but she heard him shout for the first time in her life. His arms shot out to his side as if he were able to grasp her, and then thrust above his head in jubilation. Almost as quickly, his eyes shut over his broad, twitching smile. He sat, and the happiness slowly drained from his face. The grim light of the place, the smell, the reality of her father's lost freedom settled in on her, overcame her earnest but inadequate attempts to ignore how bad things were for him at the moment, to say nothing of what lay ahead.

He was babbling. She understood when he talked about her mother, the Author, but that was all. His eyes rested when he spoke of her, so she tried to keep the subject there even though she was anxious to know about the legal proceedings. It was hard to keep him on any one topic.

"I spoke to mom yesterday—"

"The trackers they make you swallow, enormous horse pills really. Was she able to get the house back in order? How were the repairs?"

"She said things are coming back and that she's doing well under—"

"—the circumstances, yes, completely understandable. You know they make me watch the search of the house, screen it night after night, but it's—" He paused and his eyes began to dart back and forth.

"Mom explained everything. She had some friends look at the search and all the other evidence. One of them wrote a book about it, didn't even sell as many as mom's first books, so, no news screens to speak of."

Thinking of his wife and her work took him back to days after he'd lost his job. How happy he should have been. The only thing he'd done right back then was not to speak openly about his fear that the Author's work could sell. Thinking about what should have been suddenly gave him the courage to do the right thing now, the courage to more fully face the emotions he'd felt when the Girl entered the room. He moved his face so close to the barrier that she could see the heat from it color his face.

"I love you more than the world," he said, just as silence overtook him.

***

Nat came into the house of a man that he knew was of East Asian descent. But he could not tell if the man and/or his family were from what had been China, or Japan, or any of the Southeast Asian countries whose names were so vague to him now. The weight of all the things of which he was ignorant fell upon him and a great wave of anger and resentment surfaced. He hated self-pity and what he felt of it made him even angrier.

"Where are your people from?" Nat all but screamed. The man was almost too frightened to answer. He had realized almost instantly who Nat was, as no one else could have gotten past the defenses.

"What the hell does it matter? Just don't kill me for God's sake."

"You have to stop sending units to our shows. We have nothing to do with the earworm."

"Earworm? What the fuck are you talking about? I don't have any goddamn earworm. Look, I'm sorry, don't mean to be—it's nothing personal, nothing between you and me. I got a family, please, I got a family."

Something in Nat felt the need for justification. How many homes of the wealthy had he entered in the last days, weeks, months? Each of them had been connected to head-splitting violence that had happened in front of him, that cut into his sleep and made him think of prison when he was awake. He'd invaded the homes of the wealthy because there was a weight on his chest that made breathing a chore. The man in front of him was part of that weight, wasn't he? So what if he had a family? Everyone has a family: a mother and a father and all the subsequent connections.

But what if the man didn't have the worm? Nat pressed forward and probed him. But the man's obvious suffering, distorted facial features—had the others grimaced so?—and deep, wretched, involuntary noises made Nat pull back, drop the questions, and make a staggered run out of the house past groggy guards and a flickering security apparatus.

***

The Girl was in a near fetal position on the couch at her parents' home. A cup of tea steamed on the table next to her and gave the room a rich warm smell. Her mother would come into the room occasionally to check, hoping she would drink before the tea became cold.

The Girl's silence and worry became too much for her mother and she sat down next to her daughter on the couch.

"You don't know how relieved I am to have you back. If both of you had wound up in prison, I'd don't know what I'd do."

"Prison? How would I have ended up in prison?"

"You were with people that were interrogated. One of them was killed. The Revue is very close to being shut down."

"Mom, it's really hard for you to know what's really going on with Nat and Tina if you don't—"

"Anyway, that's all behind us now. I feel like I can breathe again now that you're back."

"We have to get him out."

Her mother put her head in her hands as the Girl continued. "He'll die in there. It's too much."

"Yes," the Author said, closing her eyes for a long moment. "It's all I think about. But no matter how much I spend, they spend more, and they bury us, just bury us. The insanity of your father purposely harming anyone—" She closed her eyes again. "If only there was a trace of the real killer."

Something in her mother's tone gave the Girl a flash. She sat up suddenly as she realized why there was no material trace of the killer.

"What's the matter?"

The Girl could not tell her, she didn't have the inner strength to say she would be leaving and soon, that she had to return to the Revue.

"Oh, nothing. I thought I heard something."

***

Nat came into the house with more trepidation than usual. In fact, something made him promise himself that this would be the last killing, that he would find another way to contribute to the struggle, especially since he'd seen few if any of the changes he thought he'd see. The killings had become less and less cathartic.

The house, though clearly constructed and decorated with a ridiculous amount of money, somehow avoided the decadence that had become trendy. It was as tasteful and aesthetic a place as he'd ever entered, which, at this point in his career, was saying something indeed. The rooms were large enough to contain good-sized art installations and still seem airy and light. Wall-sized screens with juxtaposed film clips from the twentieth century and from the current day (why did they skip so much?) were the main sources of light in each room.

He was startled when he realized the soft sound he heard was not from the screen, but was the noise of someone snoring and then waking up at the far end of the room. There was a woman with what might have been mathematical formulas tattooed on her arms and legs just visible below a bright orange short-sleeved top and dull green dress. She was suddenly very awake and brandishing what was probably a weapon. It seemed like a weapon, the way she pointed it at him, and by the look of utter determination combined with disgust that froze her face. He could see his face in a screen that had suddenly become visible above her. It pulsed red and flashed symbols he could not read.

"There's only one way for you to leave here alive," the woman snapped. "Carry a message back to your employer, my ex-husband, the asshole, or they will drag you out of here like the garbage you are. I want the message delivered personal, no goddamn screens. He will never get close enough to lay a hand on me again. Do you fucking hear me?"

"My employer?" Nat puzzled. "But I'm—"

Before he could say "self employed," his image disappeared from the screen, and he felt as though he'd suddenly plunged miles beneath the ocean. The pressure on every inch of his body was tremendous. His legs felt broken by the sudden weight. The blood in his nose forced him to breathe through his mouth. It all happened in a flash that seemed elongated by the pain and shock. Fortunately, he wasn't conscious very long.

***

The Girl had deeply mixed feelings about everything now, about seeing the Bird in the window of the room, what she used to think of as her room. She almost laughed at how she'd been fooled into thinking her hearing had improved because the Bird's call was so loud. Her father was out of prison and Nat was back in.

***

Nat was not fully awake, but he could hear people and music, and the two began to blend like different colored liquids mixed together until they were a new and indistinguishable color. It must have been there all the time. Why hadn't he seen it, heard it, figured out how the Old Woman talking was the Old Woman singing, was the blues in any cadence—the rhythm never left—the notes were always blue and even tinted the silence that was deeper and more open with its blueness.

Nat awoke without opening his eyes, but with a fearful smell and a familiar burning in his lungs. His head and stomach were both very clear and very sore. He did want to open his eyes because of the smell. It was different from the body odor and warm plastic smell of the prison from which he'd been released after the storm and finding the Singer, but he still knew it was prison, just different bodies and newer plastic, so he did not want to open his eyes. But he could not close his ears, though he almost wished that he could.

He could hear everything. He heard so much that for a moment he thought he may have been dreaming he was back in prison because there had never been so much—what? What could he call it but music? But it was just sound, and music was music. He played music from memory in his head and realized the curtain between those things was gone. Indeed, why had he not noticed how flimsy the curtain had always been, how shadowy and smoke like? Sound that was music, music that was sound had become something akin to light or perhaps even air and was more vivid than both. Everyone and everything had become an instrument that was in the process of tuning or playing a melody, sometimes apart, sometimes ensemble.

He thought it unwise to give in to what he feared must have been the world's dumbest smile in this place, where smiles were an invitation to disaster. He could not help himself. The sound was too much even after he opened his eyes and confirmed what he feared. His fear receded just a bit. The ceiling of the place was as low as it was in any prison and the foul stories etched in the glass walls that allowed no privacy were just as foul as ever, words that might as well have been old bloodstains, and all of it was nearly lost in what he was hearing, in the joy of sound.

***

No one cried at Nat's memorial. Tina was sedated. The Old Woman fainted and had to be carried out. It could have been that the funeral added too much weight to the interrogations she'd undergone. The Girl's head was about to explode as it raced between the relief she still felt at her father's release and the possibility that she had set the table for Nat's execution.

***

Where would she go? The Girl who was no longer a girl turned the question in her half-sleep, the question that felt like an abrasion and had kept her from solid rest all night long. The Bird had not come, but a sound woke her. No screen was open. Someone was actually at the door of the house.

"Everybody call's me LJ," the man said after the Scientist placed a cup of tea in front of him. "Like I said, I was inside with Nat. I know what he did but . . ." the man rubbed his chin and squinted as if he was trying to solve an equation.

"I knew him before the Revue, when he was just getting started. At first I was happy about the Revue, you know, cause of the publicity and what not, brought money, you know what I'm saying? Brought them goddamn units too. I was so busy counting the money and spending it, I didn't even notice at first, took my eye off the damn ball. I'd been out of there so quick.

"Anyway, they arrested the Old Woman. What the hell kinda threat is a 112-year-old? If she hadn't been dark . . . Her arrest got my attention but that was way too late. I had to resort to screens for the shows, didn't know nothing about that crap, still don't and don't wanna know. One day, this guy I hired to open the screens grows about two feet right in front of me, I mean a hundred percent brick and steel, muscles in his shit, you know what I'm saying? Anyway, he's got records of everything, but I'm still thinking, what the hell: they'll beat me, fine me, I'll get modified as best I can and go on about my business.

"Next thing I know, I'm screening Nat getting knocked out in the home of some rich, and I mean rich, woman. Then there's all kinds of probes slicing my head, never felt nothing like it, never want to feel it again. They scheduled the trial. I have to talk to six lawyers before I find one that's not connected, no company units in her family or what not. Doesn't matter.

"I wake up in a cell with Nat or in the same area with barriers; who knows how they do that shit. My head's spinning like a tornado. I know he's gonna die and I'm thinking they got me in there cause I'm gonna die too, even though they gave me years at the so-called trial. Now Nat's all calm, you know, and I'm thinking it's cause he's sorta lost his mind, the way folks get when everything crushes 'em and they sit there like they just been born.

"He's got all the death row communication privileges. You know about that? They figure everybody is too scared to be associated with condemned folks so they let you screen whoever. Mostly it's just relatives, crying and saying stuff they been holding back. But Nat's was different. Tina was the only relative. God it was good to hear her. It didn't hurt that she's beautiful and all, but that voice. She wasn't even singing real music. It was that opera stuff. Couldn't understand a damn word.

"Besides Tina, there's all these professor types and these others people in white clothes, you know the type, look like they don't walk from place to place but just float. I can only understand snatches of the conversations. Mainly, I'm waiting for Tina to come back.

"One day, I told Nat about how good her voice made me feel and asked him if he knew what she was singing. He said it was about a woman at the end of her rope, about to fall into the clutches of a real asshole, and she was singing that she had lived all her life for art and for love and that she didn't deserve none of the crap that was happening to her. I hadn't lived for art and love, but I could seriously relate.

"Before I could ask anything else, he asked me what's the difference between her singing and us talking? I thought, oh boy, the flipped out side of him is taking over. Any child knows that singing ain't talking and vice versa. Then he goes on to tell me about the Old Woman and how dark people talk like they sing and vice versa and I had to back up a bit. Yeah, I could hear the Old Woman in my head and I could hear that Billie Holiday woman Nat used to play just before he left, and I thought, he's right. They talk like they sing and vice versa. The wall between singing and talking is thinner than I thought. Nat goes on about this other old musician, Charlie Parker, and how he used notes that were really speech to show how speech was really music because everything was music and that his speed was just the flip side of Billie Holiday's slowness and easiness, same coin just turned over.

"From there it was just a hop skip to understanding, if I ever really will, why Nat was so calm. He hadn't lost his mind, or not the way folks usually lose their minds. He explained that what he had lost was the thing in his mind that allowed him to tell the difference between music and every other sound. It was all music now, a big symphony that only died down when he went to sleep.

"At first, I thought that would make it easier for him. But regardless of how calm and even happy he seemed at times, he said it saddened him more than he could say. He talked about how the last two times he walked into a rich person's home intent on probing, it had made him almost ready to confess so that he could die and wipe the confusion from his mind. He hadn't set out to kill folks. He actually just wanted to talk. But when that didn't work and the probe did, well, you know the story.

"But here he was now condemned to die and had just found more reason to live, to do the thing that he enjoyed doing most in the world: hearing, hearing like he never had before. He even said it changed how and what he saw and how he would have danced had he not been modified for death row.

"We didn't know when he was actually supposed to die. The schedules don't mean nothing nowadays. They changed the law to make it so the prisons would have 'more flexibility.' I mean, what the hell? Anyway, I'm getting more interested in his idea and I'm actually feeling it, you know, it's changing the way I hear stuff and it's making it a little easier to be there.

"Other inmates are coming to me because they can't come to Nat—the rules are nuts, don't ask me—but they're coming to me because the professors and the people with the white clothes are all over the screens talking about Nat, and how they have to save him, and how what he's discovered could revolutionize this, that, and the other. You know as soon as somebody on death row gets anything that looks like an out, they become first-class Hollywood screen action. But some of the inmates just wanted to know if it's true that me and Nat can hear everything like music because we were close to the Old Woman.

"I try to explain things as best I can that the Old Woman was a sign of something that should have been obvious to us all the time, that Billie Holiday and that Charlie Parker guy were there for us to see, or I should say to hear, and that there were others before them but they were the closest or maybe just the most obvious or maybe just the ones we knew about, not like enough people know about them, I'm just saying.

"Besides that, there was the scanner, well, not really a scanner, but a weapon they sell as a scanner; you know, rich folks can get anything tricked out. Anyway, the thing the woman used on him when he finally got zonked and caught, he thinks that what did it to him. Who knows?

"For the first time ever, I'm wanting to stay in prison cause I am finally beginning to understand, though what, I don't know. So naturally, my lawyer, God bless her dark, bookworm soul, finds a way to spring me. I should have been happy. The woman wins a major case proving that folks with unconnected lawyers are getting screwed and convicted falsely.

"Not only do I get a hard release date, but the guards start treating me like my mama never had sex. It's LJ this and LJ that. All I want to do is talk with Nat while Nat's still there to talk to.

"Other inmates are telling me it's all been planned, that I was supposed to be there with Nat and get out and spread the word about how he could hear everything for what it truly is. When I tell this to Nat, he almost laughs. He said the companies love when people say stuff that keeps the spotlight off how companies are screwing everyone raw.

LJ looked at the Woman who sat between the Author and the Scientist. "Nat said I should talk to you."

Outside Chance

I

It was so dark in the pool hall that the sunlit scene outside framed by the open door seemed like a movie of the sidewalk, the strip of grass and the traffic rather than the real thing. Rick moved in what he hoped was a casual manner toward the exit because his cousin Andre had missed in his previous two turns and was now calling for a bank shot of such exquisite difficulty that you could almost hear eyes rolling in folks' heads. Rick, on the other hand, knew the shot was a cinch for Andre, and his fear of the reaction once the ball sank into the pocket gave the already 90-degree air more charge as well as a tightness. He hoped his legs would not betray all that he was feeling as he inched toward the door.

Andre's right hand held the thick end of the cue. As he slid it back and forth, preparing the shot, it came tantalizingly close to a wad of rubber-banded bills that sat on the thick polished wooden edge of the pool table. The money was the wager Andre was about to snap up, a big sucker bet that contained the better part of some poor sap's weekly check.

Said sap sat smiling, sipping suds under one of the many plastic cone-shaped lamps that hung from the ceiling. Andre, in his twenties, was in pretty good shape, but he still wondered if he could make the shot, pick up the money, and move to the door before things got ugly, prohibitively ugly.

It had been easier than he thought to recruit his younger cousin Rick to the scam. Rick had always come across to him as a bookworm and a do-gooder. He'd introduced Andre to movies you had to read because the actors didn't speak English. Even if they had, things they did made no sense and couldn't hold Andre's attention for very long.

"Why would anyone want to go to a movie where you watch somebody read?" he'd asked Rick in an almost too loud voice during a Godard film. "We took two buses to watch a movie where people went on vacation and read books."

On the way back from the film it was late and the bus was nearly empty. They commandeered the back bench seats and propped up their feet.

"You know you owe me," Andre chided Rick, "for forcing me to see that shitty movie, no action, no sex, no nothing."

"What do you mean no action? What about how they treated one another; doesn't that count?"

Andre looked skyward, palmed the top of Rick's head, raised his other hand and pleaded, "God, help this boy see the light. Let him understand the difference between talk and action." They both laughed.

"If you want action, come with me to the demonstration against the war," Rick retorted.

"You know JB was on Ed Sullivan tonight," Andre said before breaking into song. "I got the feeling!"

"So you don't want to go to the march?"

"That's just a bunch of white folks making noise," Andre said dismissively and turned toward the back window.

But, even as he spoke, Andre thought of how he dreaded seeing the mail truck parked on his street. He tried not to think about the draft, fearing he would jinx the whole deal. Somehow, at least so far, he'd escaped. No Army notice had appeared in his mailbox calling him to a jungle battlefield in a country he'd never heard of before the war. Others he knew had not been so lucky.

He recalled Wilson's homecoming party. Wilson was a guy who had terrorized Andre and many others well into high school. Wilson made sure everyone knew he carried a knife. Those who had seen him use it talked about it, but never on the witness stand.

Wilson's welcome-back party had featured the typical loud music that greeted you at the doorstep. Streamers and balloons were taped to the porch. Andre knew something was up when he opened the door and saw no one dancing. There was a knot of people around the bathroom, which wouldn't have been unusual except that, even over the music, he could hear what he thought was the guest of honor cursing on the other side of the door. "It's that bag they attached to him," complained a girl he didn't recognize. "It doesn't work sometimes. It's that damn bag."

"I'll go to the demonstration if you come with me to the pool hall and keep an eye out," Andre had offered.

"An eye out for what?"

"Better yet, shoot a game with me."

"You've got to be joking."

"You will win, guaranteed," Andre smiled.

That's what Rick had been afraid of, but something in Andre's easy manner enticed him to be part of the plan, to stay connected. He also didn't want to imagine Andre in the pool hall without backup, trying to work a hustle. Though his experience with such things was limited, Rick had tried to push his fear down somewhere he couldn't feel it. It made his throat tight and dry.

Minutes before they had entered the pool hall, Andre had dropped more details about the escape plan they might need after the trap had been sprung. Rick was now in the early phase of that loose plan, close to the door, making sure, as much as anyone could, that no one blocked it. He didn't understand how he was supposed to do that and remain inconspicuous.

As Rick had feared, the man sitting under the cone lamp had become a bit upset after Andre made the nearly impossible bank shot and summarily stuffed the wad of cash into his pocket. The man rose from his seat slowly, his jaw tighter than a submarine hatch. Worse yet, he was looking back and forth between Rick and Andre. During one of his glances over at Andre, Rick took the opportunity to bolt. When the man turned to see Rick fleeing into the sunlight, Andre jumped over the bar and shot out the back.

Rounding the corner to meet Rick, Andre smiled as they trotted until they heard footsteps and saw not one, but three men racing toward them. One of them had what looked like a metal pipe.

"You take the alley. I'll take the street," Andre panted.

This was a change in the plan that left Rick cold. Andre was supposed to run down the alley if they had to split up. Rick was from Detroit and didn't know DC well enough not to get lost once he left familiar streets. But the men chasing them were closer, and even though there was a rock in one of his shoes that were not made for running (why hadn't he worn his sneakers?), this was no time for questions. He did not even look back to see the source of the pounding feet and curses that followed him to the alley.

He managed to put distance between him and his pursuers, turn left back on the sidewalk, and duck into a street level apartment with an unlocked screen door. There was a closet in the room to his right. He jumped in and shut the door seconds after he heard someone else open the screen door.

Rick was trying so hard to quiet his breathing he thought he'd pass out. Someone came down a flight of stairs, close to the closet. A woman spoke nervously to the man who'd just chased Rick to the apartment.

"Wow, you just walked into my pad?" she said, sounding white to Rick's ears.

"I'm looking for somebody," the man panted, "just robbed me."

"What are you talking about?"

Another set of footsteps fast and heavy could be heard on the stairs.

"At the pool hall, guy just cheated me out of—"

"Whoever it is ain't here, so just split," a man's voice interrupted him.

There was silence, then footsteps going away.

"What the hell was that about?"

"Some crap at the pool hall. I'm glad you woke up."

"I'm glad it wasn't serious. Things are just beginning to—"

The sudden silence took Rick's breath away. Oddly, he noticed that he'd been smelling expensive marijuana and cheap incense.

Before he could notice anything else, the closet doorknob rattled and the door swung open.

Rick didn't even look up. He put his head down and pushed off the back wall with one foot. The man was knocked to the ground. The woman jumped back. Was she reaching for something in the drawer?

Rick was in the doorway, but the man leapt from the floor and was on him, two sinuous arms around Rick's waist, wrestling. The man dropped one arm only to throw a punch that missed and grazed Rick's ear with a nasty sting.

"Tyrone, don't. He's just a boy," the woman shouted. He had Rick against the wall.

"I was just hiding. I swear to God. I had to hide."

"You came damn close to hiding in a hole in the ground."

The woman sat and exhaled. She was pregnant. She and the man could have been brother and sister. He was a shade darker but with long, straight hair.

"You scared the crap out of me. I thought I was going to have it right then."

"Please, I haven't done anything. I just want to go home."

"Come and sit down and tell us what the hell is going on." The woman pushed a kitchen chair toward him with her foot. "I think you owe us that much."

Rick sat, feeling the unsteadiness in his legs just as he made contact with the chair.

"You look pretty young to be cheating someone out of their money."

"How do you know he was cheated?" Rick asked. "Sometimes, you just lose."

Tyrone smiled despite himself.

***

"They charge a lot of money for these papers?" Andre tried to ask in a nonchalant way.

"It depends," Rick replied. "If Tyrone has to write the paper, they charge more than if they just buy it already written from another student."

"But how does the student that's buying the paper know? He should charge everybody based on how many pages are in the paper."

"You can be his business manager."

"Sounds like somebody needs to."

"The folks from the pool hall can't be still looking for us," Rick said, changing the subject. "I didn't come here to spend my summer inside."

"You want to spend it in the hospital? Besides, the Smithsonian ain't going nowhere. Tell me about this Tyrone and the Schwartz guy too."

"Schwartz is actually a woman, pregnant, as a matter of fact."

"OK, but what about the operation?"

"What difference does it make? You don't even like to read subtitles. How are you going to help crank out papers to sell?"

"You pay to read subtitles. He gets paid for the papers. That's a whole other world."

***

On his second visit to Tyrone and Schwartz's, Rick got high and had sex. He had seen people when they were drunk and/or high and had read about the effect of psychoactives: cannabis leaf, hashish, LSD, mushrooms, and the like. He had noted the similarities between the more intense psychedelic experiences and meditation. But this was the thing itself.

Time puzzled him. It suddenly seemed like he'd always been high and had simply failed to realize it. The moments when

Tyrone had gone upstairs to write and Schwartz had turned to Rick smiling and lit a joint and asked him if he'd ever felt a baby moving all collapsed into the moment his ear was on her stomach, and then, thoughtless and clear, he turned his lips to brush against the gentle swell.

When had she actually handed him the cigarette? It was warm. Why had it surprised him that something lit on one end and that she had been holding on the other end was warm? He inhaled, choked, drank some water and tried again. The upright chair in the kitchenette that had been utterly comfortable a moment ago now seemed to urge him to sit on the softer, tiny couch near the stairs.

There, the title of a book—*Black No More*—caught his attention. It looked old and, as he began to read it, he was amazed that it had been published in the 1930s. It began with a black man, the apparent protagonist, who paid to turn himself white using a method developed by a black scientist whose aim was to get rid of racism in the US. The man who paid to become white made the change in no small part to pursue a white woman who wouldn't go out with black men. Racial identities leap-frogged over and over in Rick's head and then exchanged themselves in some sort of mirror and took him back to Schwartz.

She turned on the radio. Strange rock music smeared itself into the smell of the smoke in the room. He chuckled hearing the obviously white singer say "Lord have mercy." He didn't know white people even knew the phrase existed. Then there was the curious refrain, "white light, white heat."

It seemed to her like he'd been reading forever, though he was flipping pages faster than even she could have done. She tried to use her fascination with watching him read to replace the other thoughts that rose in her like a swift current. He was underage, right? If she asked him how old he was and he lied or confirmed what she feared, what then?

She saw his eyes when she closed her eyes as he had moaned against her stomach and the vibration made her wet. She did not want to admit that being pregnant had made her want sex in a way she never had before. She also had not wanted to admit that she missed her lover, nor that the only thing that dampened her anger at what her brother had done to him was the memory of making love in a space cleared in the woods. She told herself smoking marijuana would calm her disruptions and urges but suspected that was close to being a lie.

How old was he, really, this boy plowing through the novel? It seemed like he'd been reading forever.

Whatever happened would be alright, she thought. The apartment was temporary. Everything in that place was just for a time.

When he looked up from the book to ask her the question reading had given him the courage to ask—why was her name Schwartz?—she was unbuttoning her blouse and walking towards him.

***

After having sex for the first time while being high for the first time, it took every ounce of self restraint for Rick to try not to go back the very next day very early in the morning. She had told him it was best if they remained "discreet."

As far as Rick was concerned, "discretion" also meant going back alone, without Andre. Though it took a lot to convince Andre not to accompany him on his third visit to Tyrone and Schwartz's place.

"It's still new. I am working things out. It's delicate because of the way I rushed in there and everything," Rick worked to persuade his cousin. He had to promise over and over to mention Andre's idea about charging per page and to tell whose idea it had been.

Even before he'd made love with Schwartz, Rick wanted the visits to himself to talk books. He couldn't imagine Andre talking anything but business. He wondered why Andre was adamant about being part of the academic paper scheme. For that matter, he began to question his own motivation.

He had never been part of anything illegal or even unseemly until that summer. Was it the money? Certainly, he had never had as much money as the pool hall split with Andre. The paper mill hustle was different from the pool hustle but it was still a hustle, albeit one that was now conflated in Rick's mind with seduction. Rick was unsure of where the college paper scheme was in terms of legality and didn't feel up to asking. The prospect of another hustle ending in fiasco did not encourage him. He could still feel where the sharp pebbles from the alley had dug into his feet while he ran desperately from the pool hall pursuers. His shoes had taken a beating and he remembered how his hands shook even after he'd been sitting for a while.

Hustle or no, he glowed at the idea of spending time with Schwartz and Tyrone. He'd never talked about Ann Petry or William Faulkner with anyone outside of class. The couple seemed to live with books the way his family and friends lived with music. He'd also never before considered a pregnant woman attractive, and then there was her voice. He remembered how during his accidental first visit she sang a Marvelettes' song as Tyrone poured their tea. In the song, tables are turned, reality shifts, and the world becomes a new place as it had become with his escape into their small, jerry-rigged apartment.

Tyrone had smiled as if he had just closed his mouth over the last sweet crust of peach cobbler.

"That's one of *those* songs," he'd said.

Rick look at him expectantly.

"He means," Schwartz spoke up, "it's code, not really a love song."

"Robert Johnson was the master of that, baby!" Tyrone said beaming. "All those songs about the Devil, and stuff like "Hellhound on my Trail." If you told the straight truth back then, you didn't shame the Devil, you called him out of his lair followed by the lynch mob."

"Oh yes," Schwartz said, rolling her eyes, "I'm sure the Marvelettes were really singing about turning the tables on the White Citizens' Councils."

Rick had gone to the bathroom after several cups of tea and walked out with a copy of *Native Son* he found on the shelf with stacks of toilet paper, anti-war protest flyers, and paperback copies of *Hamlet* and Ellison's *Invisible Man*.

"You like the bleak stuff?" Tyrone said, nodding at the Wright novel.

"Hamlet is bleak too, no conflict, no motivation," Rick replied.

"No motivation! You don't know what the hell you're talking about," Tyrone smirked.

"I know it's only people who've got their behinds on pillows with nothing better to do who sit around wondering whether life is worth living. Everyone else is too busy trying to live."

A mocking laugh almost caused Schwartz to spit out her tea. "Tyrone used to say the same thing," she said, looking directly at him, "until I showed him all the father figures in the play."

"Yeah," Tyrone agreed grudgingly. "It's not 'to be or not to be.' It's about who's your daddy, the dead father, the usurper king . . ."

"Laertes," Rick added, suddenly coming to a realization.

***

Essentially, there was no third visit to Tyrone and Schwartz's
even though Rick came prepared with a list of books and literary questions to discuss. He'd put that in his pocket. In his
wallet, he'd folded the start of a love letter. He'd dreamt he was
home with Schwartz on Belle Isle on a blanket beneath a tree,
eating fruit as she sang.

The reality check came when he was a block away from their
place. Two black "unmarked" police cars were parked in front.
He crossed the street and decided to observe discreetly. Closer,
he saw Schwartz at the door talking to two beefy white, uni-
formed cops and two more in plain clothes. He walked by,
fighting the urge to look directly at them. Resisting that urge
fell in line with everything Rick had learned about how to act
when the police stop you, what to watch for, down to whether
or not the small strip of leather over the butt of the holstered
gun was snapped or unsnapped, readied.

"Never, ever look at the gun until the cop is looking at your
ID," he heard Andre's voice in his head.

He turned to see what was happening when he thought he
heard Schwartz's voice catch and release in what sounded like
a sob.

***

It was near night when the police finally tired of Schwartz's
silence and decided to let her leave the precinct. Besides, they
felt they had her brother cold and he was their target. She left
the police station but was not free. She felt tied to the jail as
if she was evacuating a disaster leaving her brother behind.
She would have to call her mother, after all this time, with bad
news. She wished it was later, that sleep would come sooner,

that the city night would deliver stars as intoxicating as the ones she'd seen in Virginia. At the same time, she wished she'd never set foot in the woods near the cabin.

II

Schwartz had never thought of paradise as having night until she'd spent a few evenings with her new lover out in the open, staring at the sky. She didn't know or care about the constellations like he did, but she loved to hear him talk about what he called "signs of heaven," his voice cool and colorless as the stream. He was plain spoken and smiled at the slightest provocation, red bow lips on pale skin. The stars they shared were static fireworks, a painting of white Christmas bulbs flung out on endless black. He was happy to show her what he kept calling "the real sky," away from the city.

He had first seen her walking in and out of sunlight by a nameless creek beneath a stand of trees in unnaturally straight rows, river birches with their ever-peeling, cinnamon-red barks with dull orange undersides that reminded him of sunburn-flaked skin. Her walk was aimless. He couldn't tell if she was bored or amused. She wasn't local. She may not have been from Virginia at all. That made her beauty all the more exotic. He had once seen a Swedish actress on the cover of a magazine with lips as thick as hers. She was not quite as pale as the actress but her amazingly curly hair was just as gold.

Her mother had rented an isolated cabin for the week. Her brother was supposed to join them for the long weekend when he could get off work. They had all planned to do nothing but read during the day and talk about what they read when it got dark. The cabin had no electricity. The brother was late.

When Schwartz finally introduced the young man she had met in the woods to her mother, she looked at him with a curious smile. Schwartz recognized the expression from when she was young and had presented her mother with a drawing or homemade gift that her mother couldn't quite make out. The mother wondered if Schwartz and the young man were lovers or would become lovers. Though the lovers knew the answer, they didn't know a child was coming.

***

Tyrone had been in a panic because he'd delayed his reading assignment and subsequent paper due the Wednesday after the long weekend. He'd gotten off work early and thought he would just scan the book to get a feel for it but, to his surprise, *Paradise Lost* was a page turner, from the psychedelic fire of creation to the unexpectedly nuanced and tortured Satan, a sort of cosmic film noir protagonist. Eve had just arrived on the scene when Tyrone noticed the sun was low and realized he was supposed to have been on the road to the cabin some time ago.

He had to stop reading. It felt unnatural for him to leave the world he'd entered, as if something had been pulled out of socket, dislocated. The purple clouds on the horizon, magnificent as they were, loomed as sudden threats. He hadn't finished packing. He was supposed to have asked the man down the street about the rattling noise in the car's gearbox.

The last thing he'd wanted was to try to find the cabin in the dark, but it was almost two am when he arrived. He slept in while Schwartz and his mother fixed breakfast and read. He awoke groggily, ate cold eggs, and eventually learned that Schwartz had a new boyfriend. He laughed sardonically at the discovery.

"There's another black family out here?" he asked half rhetorically.

The mother sighed. Earlier, she'd almost been happy that Tyrone was late, that he hadn't been there when Schwartz had brought the young man to the cabin. It had allowed her another day to avoid the issue or think there might be a time when she could bring it up with Schwartz before Tyrone's arrival. Would things have been more difficult but somehow simpler if her darker child had been present when Schwartz's young man was introduced? Would the young white man have filled in the gaps?

"Honey, your brother's got a point. Did you tell the young man? You know what he probably thinks. Seeing me didn't help any."

"How do you know he even cares about it, that it even matters?"

"A white boy, in Virginia no less, who doesn't care about race?" Tyrone said incredulously. "Be for real."

Schwartz dropped her book and walked swiftly out of the cabin into the woods.

"You've got to go easier with her, Tyrone. She doesn't see things as . . . clearly as you, sometimes."

He reached for his mother's hand, looked to the woods where Schwartz had disappeared, and reluctantly realized he needed to talk with her.

"How do you know he doesn't know?" Schwartz asked defensively.

"How many black people have blond hair and pale skin?"

"My lips are thick as yours and you can't even have a fro."

"There are white people with fros these days, in case you haven't noticed." He had not wanted to become agitated. He knew they were on the one subject that could take his sister over the edge. But he couldn't stop himself and began talking emphatically with his hands.

"Most white people are not like—"

"Don't give me that 'mom is the exception to the rule' crap for the umpteenth time," she said angrily, mocking his hand movement.

"Be for real!" he shouted. "Look at the world. I didn't make it. Did I drag people over here in chains?"

Sitting outside the cabin, she hoped no one could hear her children shouting. She was about to go inside when she heard gunfire echoing from the woods. The shots opened a chasm of fear and regret from an unclosed wound, the death of her husband.

***

She had met her husband, a wiry, tan-skinned, handsome man with thick glasses, at the University of Michigan bookstore a year after the bombing of Pearl Harbor. She was a cashier and he held court with a handful of other Negroes (were there more than that on campus? why had she not noticed them before?) in a lounge just beyond the checkout counter. He had tales of a bohemian weekend in New York and the politics of the new bebop jazz movement. But it was his knowledge of opera that fascinated her. That was an art of both magic and privilege, a harbor. They spent their rare leisure hours in the library's listening room, worlds away from where they sat.

People stared, but just as many remarked that they made a beautiful couple. They managed to find a justice of the peace willing to conduct a small civil ceremony and then embarked on a visit to astonished, apprehensive, but mostly cordial relatives. Reluctantly, he agreed they would go south to visit his oldest relative.

"I'll get to meet your great-grandmother, finally."

"Let's hope that's not the operative term," he had replied.

His great-grandmother was bedridden in rural Alabama, where marriages such as his were tantamount to attacking the local Ku Klux Klan. The now obvious pregnancy (with what turned out to be twins) did not mitigate the situation. The image she would always hold of the great-grandmother was of her eyes. When the elderly woman saw the two of them together for the first time, her eyes widened, then narrowed. There was no malice. It was as if the old woman was trying to read something barely fathomable.

On his way to the closest grocery store, miles from the house, her husband had called from a gas station to say he was having car trouble. She never heard from him again. The car was found torched. Diplomatic but insistent inquiries from the University newspaper and her husband's doctoral committee prompted authorities to conduct a nominal investigation. Services were held without the body.

***

Tyrone had pushed Schwartz to the ground after the first shot. After the second blast, he was overcome and ran toward where the shots rang out. She looked up and shouted his name just as she saw someone with a rifle turn and dart through the trees. The flash of the face she saw stabbed at her heart.

He was almost out of ammo and the colored boy was coming for him, moving with the legendary swiftness he thought those people had. Would his fleeing make him seem less of a hero to her? He knew the woods. Surely, a few twist and turns would leave the black bastard in the dust. He miscalculated.

206 kim d. hunter

Catching a glint of sun on the gun barrel edging through the knot of a tree, Tyrone crouched and, despite his anger, almost laughed to himself. He could hear his mother telling him the story of a changeling being left in a tree, traded for a human baby.

"I got your changeling," he thought and gritted his teeth. The ground was soft with moss. Only the occasional faint snap of a twig betrayed his movement and he left plenty of time between those sounds.

When he'd seen it was a white boy shooting, he knew it was his sister's lover and that she would be torn by the assault. But that somehow made him all the more furious. It took him back to the process of slowly learning why his father was not around.

Their mother had carefully fed them age-appropriate bits of information until one afternoon, when it all collapsed into the ugly truth of a body burned beyond recognition. It had left the three of them with an unspeakable bond.

Tyrone managed to surprise him from behind, but not before the white man in the hollow tree pulled the gun from where it had been pointing. He tried to re-aim, but Tyrone was on him. They were bloodied in the struggle before the gun went off.

Later, Tyrone lied to his mother and sister and said he'd been outrun. They would be leaving the next morning anyway.

Months later, when the police came to their mother's door, she told them she didn't know where her son or daughter were. The circles beneath her eyes caused the police to pity her and suspect she was lying. She didn't tell what little she knew, that something terrible must have happened to cause her son to leave with no explanation and for her daughter, denying pregnancy, to insist on going with him. As much as anything, their false cheerfulness had disturbed their mother's sleep.

***

Schwartz and her brother were looking for a fresh start, albeit in the city of their birth, where their mother had moved in with in-laws after her husband's murder. Though she had eventually moved them all back to Detroit because the factories paid more than the universities, Tyrone and Schwartz knew enough about DC to pretend they'd always lived there, that they had not arrived from a distance with a story.

On the long bus trip to the nation's capital, they had argued over the question of making a living. Details eluded them. It always ended in the same place—something menial until something better came along.

The apartment they rented had once clearly been some sort of store. The door opened directly onto the sidewalk: no steps, lawn, or porch. The bathroom was tiny and the shower jerry-rigged into place. She found it functional but, though he tried to hide it, it depressed Tyrone deeply—not so much the physical place but that it had come to this, that he would be lucky to stay out of prison, to say nothing of fulfilling his dreams. Despite her misgivings about spending money they didn't have, she agreed to go to the bar with him after they'd stored their meager belongings.

The place, a few blocks from the university, was crowded, but they managed to find a table. He went to stand in one of the lines at the bar to order. He returned to find his sister talking with a white couple at the next table. They tried to hide their surprise seeing Tyrone sit down with what they had assumed was a white woman. They were equally surprised and a bit relieved to notice the incredible resemblance between the two.

"I know how you feel," the young man was saying to Schwartz as Tyrone sat down. "We should both be back at the dorm working on the same doggone paper."

The woman with him, close to being drunk, almost sputtered, "It's so stupid, though. I mean I can't even tell my mom. She would be so pissed-off to know that I have to write about a brother and sister having sex, even if it is in an opera."

"*Sigmund und Sieglinde*," Schwartz piped up. "Actually, their incest is *supposed* to be an outrage; it's the result of, well, it's a long story, as I'm sure you know, but it's not glorified or anything."

"Wow, are you opera fans or something?" the man asked.

"It was our dad's dissertation," Tyrone said with a sad smile.

"Can we call your dad?" the woman said with a look that was half joke and half desperation.

"He's dead."

"Sorry to hear that. We uh . . ."

"He died before we were born."

"Oh, God," the woman frowned.

"We're gonna stop bugging you now," the man said, looking slightly embarrassed.

"Wait," the woman interrupted. She placed both hands on the table and mustered as serious an expression as she could under the circumstances. "You've obviously read the dissertation. How fast can you write? We can pay."

III

Rick saw Schwartz walking towards the house from the bus stop. The closer she got, the sadder she looked.

"What's the matter?" He was afraid to ask about Tyrone. He felt a low gray ceiling descending over the summer. Without

Tyrone and Schwartz, Rick would be constrained to the pool halls where Andre had not run scams, and the sections of the Smithsonian where Andre's status as a guard allowed Rick free access, all of which Rick had already thoroughly perused.

Even though he had refused Tyrone's pleas to help churn out papers, he had actually begun writing a paper for a business student taking a philosophy course, comparing Hamlet and Bigger Thomas, entitled "Choosing a Course of Action Even When There Seems to Be No Choice." He had wanted to return to Schwartz and Tyrone's because he wanted to talk books. He told himself writing the paper was the price of admission.

"Did they tear the place up?"

"You know they did! And he didn't even try to hide. He gave himself up because . . ."

She looked down, her hands on either side of her face. "He didn't want them to harm me."

"Did they find the stuff he wrote, I mean the memoirs and the play, *The Report*?"

"Who the hell cares? They weren't there because of what he wrote."

Rick only had the slightest clue as to why the police would be after Tyrone, things Tyrone had muttered when he was really high.

***

Andre had been assigned to the new part of the museum, a theater where they reenacted the trial of John Brown. He was looking forward to it, a much welcomed break in the monotony. He was standing near the turnstiles, waiting for more detailed instructions from his supervisor, when he noticed a group of men approaching. Some were in wheelchairs; some were in military uniform. A young, black, nearly bald GI ran to catch up with them and approached Andre, smiling.

"Got a bunch of vets here on field day." He handed Andre about a dozen tickets.

"The ticket taker isn't here yet, she's—"

He recognized Wilson in a wheelchair and walked over to him. The man in the chair looked up, unsmiling but not unfriendly.

"Hey, man. How's it going?"

"How the hell does it look like it's going?"

"I didn't mean anything like that. I—"

Wilson dropped his head. "I know you didn't."

He reached into his breast pocket, unfolded a piece of paper, looked at it, and handed it to Andre. It had the time, date and place for the anti-war march.

***

Andre didn't get home until long after dark and Rick could tell he had been drinking. He wasn't as funny as usual. After Rick introduced him to Schwartz, Andre joked in his best Butterfly McQueen voice that he "don't know nothin' 'bout birthin' no babies," then remarked that white folks wouldn't understand the joke about the joke. When that was met with silence, he stared at Schwartz for a moment.

"You're not . . ."

"My mother is!" she snapped.

"Don't get mad at me. It's dark, I've had a couple of shots, and it's been a long day, all right? I assume a lot's been happening 'cause you're here without your husband."

"He's her brother, not her husband. There's stuff I need to tell you."

"Tell me in the morning. I'm going to bed. You and me are going to the anti-war march and they start gathering early. You can come too if you want," he said to Schwartz.

***

Andre woke up before everyone else and fixed breakfast. Rick came down and Andre began talking about Wilson. They were about to walk out of the door when Schwartz came down. She seemed somehow more pregnant than the night before and had to convince the two guys that walking was good for a pregnant woman.

They walked over to the stadium and got on the bus that would take them to the National Mall. The bus was already packed with young white people. It seemed all the men had long hair. Some of them stared at the trio of Andre, Rick, and Schwartz as they paid their fares. A woman got up to let Schwartz take a seat. One young man thought she looked familiar, but when he realized where he knew her from, decided to stay silent.

None of them had ever been to a protest march before, to say nothing of one that large. Schwartz first learned about it because Tyrone paid to have some of the flyers printed. Rick had first read about it in an underground paper he found on a table in the Museum cafeteria while he waited for Andre's shift to end. They saw dozens, then hundreds of people walking to the National Mall. They arrived overwhelmed by what seemed like millions.

The crowd was overwhelmingly white, as Andre had expected. The few black men he saw made him think of Wilson handing him the flyer from a wheel chair. The image wore on him. He zoned out during the speeches. After buying a Black Panther paper from a woman he knew, he was besieged by white people trying to sell him other papers. He was very ready to leave.

Schwartz was the one who noticed Rick was missing. She began looking for him as Andre tried to convince her they needed a plan find his cousin. She made it to the edge of the crowd where the police presence was evident. Andre was beginning to feel the effects of the previous night's drinking and to question why the hell he was there with this white looking black woman he barely knew. Suddenly, he couldn't even remember her name.

"Hey, hey wait," he shouted.

But she couldn't hear as she approached a police officer to ask if there were somewhere lost minors were gathered. Another cop who had seen them emerging from the crowd assumed Andre was an unwanted pursuer, approached, and shoved him to the ground. Andre hopped to his feet as the crowd around him gave way and two other cops rushed in for backup.

Acknowledgments

Any fault you find with this text rests with the so-called author. All that engages you is the result of the collaborative effort of the following gracious people: Tyrone Williams, Karla Passalacqua, Jane Slaughter, Dennis Teichman, Peter Markus, Melba Joyce Boyd, Chris Tysh, M. L. Liebler, Rick Ward, Annie Martin and the entire wonderful team at Wayne State University Press, my family Kathryn Savoie and Anika Hunter for putting up with my hours away from them as well as for their deep listening, and my mother for seeds from decades ago that remain.

About the Author

kim d. hunter has published two collections of poetry: *borne on slow knives and edge of the time zone.* His poetry appears in *Rainbow Darkness, What I Say, Black Renaissance Noire, 6X6* #35, and elsewhere.

He received a 2012 Kresge Artist Fellowship in the Literary Arts and he works in Detroit providing media support to social justice groups.